Samuel John Stone

Lays of Iona and other poems

Samuel John Stone

Lays of Iona and other poems

ISBN/EAN: 9783337206819

Printed in Europe, USA, Canada, Australia, Japan

Cover: Foto ©Andreas Hilbeck / pixelio.de

More available books at **www.hansebooks.com**

LAYS OF IONA

AND OTHER POEMS

BY

S. J. STONE, M.A.

RECTOR OF ALL-HALLOWS'-ON-THE-WALL, E.C.

AUTHOR OF 'THE KNIGHT OF INTERCESSION,' ETC.

' Deum patrem ingenitum coeli ac terrae dominum
Ab eodemque filium secula ante primogenitum
Deumque spiritum sanctum verum unum altissimum
Invoco ut auxilium mihi opportunissimum
Minimo praestet omnium sibi deservientium.'

(From the Antiphon of the *Altus Prosator*
of St. Columba. See pp. 174, 175.)

LONGMANS, GREEN AND CO.

39 PATERNOSTER ROW, LONDON

NEW YORK AND BOMBAY

1897

DEDICATED

TO MY DEAR SISTER

SARAH HARRIETTE BOYD

CONTENTS

DR. JOHNSON'S JOURNEY TO IONA
IN 1773

' WE were now treading that illustrious Island which
was once the luminary of the Caledonian regions—
whence savage clans and roaming barbarians derived
the benefits of Knowledge and the blessings of
Religion.   To abstract the mind from all local
emotion would be impossible, if it were endeavoured,
and would be foolish if it were possible.   Whatever
withdraws us from the power of our senses,—whatever makes the past, the distant, or the future
predominate over the present, advances us in the
dignity of thinking beings.   Far from me and from
my friends be such frigid philosophy as may conduct
us indifferent and unmoved over any ground which
has been dignified by wisdom, bravery, or virtue.
That man is little to be envied whose patriotism
would not gain force upon the plain of Marathon,
or whose piety would not grow warmer among the
Ruins of Iona.'

PREFACE

Bishop Ewing, in his *Account of the Early Celtic Church and the Mission of Saint Columba*, says that few things are finer (all hackneyed as they are) than the apostrophe of the Saxon pilgrim, Dr. Samuel Johnson, which he wrote on landing on the shores of Iona: and he states his belief that these famous lines have done almost as much for Iona, in modern times, as the writings of Sir Walter Scott for Scotland.

There is perhaps enough truth in this opinion to justify the insertion of the well-known passage on the preceding page.

Nevertheless, it must be admitted that any real interest in Iona did not generally exist until late in this nineteenth century. Even now, though popular knowledge of the Island and of the Celtic Church has so increased that the number of English people who have hazy notions as to the difference between Columba and Columbus, and who have never even heard of St. Aidan, has sensibly diminished, anything like thorough acquaintance with the subject is confined to a few. Such extension of knowledge as does obtain is to be traced, doubtless, not only to the increased interest in the history of the Church generally, but especially to the desire of the children of the Church of England to know more about their own spiritual ancestry.

In that particular direction the interest has been chiefly the growth of the last thirty years.

In the year 1872 the Author of this work published a volume entitled *The Knight of Intercession, and other Poems*. One of these poems was the 'Lay of St. Columb of Iona,' which is reproduced now at page 185. When that volume came to a third edition, the Author, wishing to include some more recent poems and yet not to increase the size of the book, removed such pieces of the first edition as he thought had roused but little attention. This ballad was one of those he omitted, as being least attractive in subject.

He was at first greatly surprised to find that a number of his earlier readers expressed publicly or privately much regret at the removal of these

Iona verses : but the evident increase of interest in all the Church history of that period, which had been quietly growing, explained to him later on the principal cause of this regret, for the poem itself was but slight and not largely according to knowledge.

This fact, and several subsequent visits to the Island (which he had not seen when the earlier verses were written), and a fuller personal acquaintance with the whole subject, have resulted in the writing and publication of these new poems, as well as in the re-insertion of the omitted ballad, with various necessary corrections and a few additions.

This late birth or revival of interest in the subject of the Celtic ancestry of the Anglican Church has not unnaturally led to some controversy, in which on one side the debt of that Church to the Gregorian Mission has been comparatively minimised, and on the other—by a reaction easily to be understood—the mighty claims of the Celtic Church on our filial reverence and gratitude have either been reduced to the smallest proportions, or grudgingly conceded.

The convictions of the Author of this volume, derived from all the sources of historical knowledge and opinion upon both sides which have been within his reach, are in the direction of the views expressed, most notably perhaps, by the late Bishop of Durham, Dr. Lightfoot; but they are qualified by a strong feeling that while on the one hand the comparative debt of England to the Mission from Iona is far the highest and the deepest in a directly spiritual point of view, yet on the other she owes much, in particulars of great importance, to the benefits she has received from her connection with the Italian Mission. Apart from that connection, it is difficult to understand that the Anglican Church could now present, and could hope to present still more largely in future, the front of settled order and effective organisation, and the aspect of dignity, culture, and learning, which are as characteristic of her at her best as are her noble love of truth and her devout and pure enthusiasm.

But all this being allowed, he thinks it cannot be doubted that those historical and critical authorities, such as Montalembert, Bishop Lightfoot, and many other moderns of the highest intellectual rank, are in the right, who maintain that—as regards the spirit and heart of religion and the noblest and purest principles of missionary work—however great and real is the debt to the Mission by St. Augustine, and however much is owing to earlier British sources of evangelisation—the chief debt of Anglo-Saxon Christianity is due to the Celtic Church and its Fathers. In the highest sense, therefore, the cradle of our branch of the Catholic Church is to be identified with the two holy Islands of Iona and Lindisfarne, and with the names of St. Columba and St. Aidan and their spiritual sons, more than with those of St. Augustine and his followers—truly honoured and gratefully remembered as these Gregorian Missionaries ought to be.

The pure Celtic blood in our spiritual ancestry explains and justifies many peculiarities of the Anglican Church in position and in opinion.

It explains and justifies the fact that, by her Catholic loyalty to primitive apostolical order and sacerdotal and sacramental doctrine, she is as distinct from any form of Presbyterianism or English Nonconformity on the one hand, as on the other hand, by her stern purity in rejection of un-Catholic accretions and corruptions, she is removed from later mediæval and modern Romanism.

So, too, is to be understood the objection which the English Church has from time to time manifested to Papal domination, even when in those later mediæval times she was so much under its power:—the clerical chafing and lay impatience and general discomfort so frequently in evidence under the thrall of the 'later Roman.'

Moreover, it explains and justifies her own Reformation in principle, though not of course in every particular and as regards every agency.

A strong conviction that all this is of manifest historical truth, and that it is of much importance that the sons and daughters of the Catholic Church of England generally should be helped in every possible way to realise intelligently what they owe to the pure parent spirit of the Celtic Church, and to look gratefully to the principal Rock from which they have been hewn, has led the Author of this volume to the writing of the greater part of its contents in the earnest hope that the poems may serve to this end, be it ever so slightly, and as the work of one who is himself a learner.   A great

attraction, especially, towards the characters of St.
Columba and St. Aidan, and, too, a personal love
for the Island of Iona itself, increased by a close
acquaintance with it—made easy to him by the most
kind hospitality and encouragement of the Bishop of
Argyll and the Isles—have had their strong influence
over the writer: but he has had most at heart a
devout and reverent regard for that spirit of the
Celtic Church—the spirit of pure Catholic truth, of
simple devotion, of holy peace, of self-denying power
and zeal, of deep personal love for our Lord and the
souls for whom He died—which he has endeavoured
to represent in those verses entitled 'The Spirit of
the Church from Iona,' which precede this poem,
and strike the keynote of the whole work.

. . . . .

There are several points to which it seems desir-
able, before the close of this Preface, to make some
individual reference.

(1) It will probably seem to some critics that the
poem is overloaded with notes. The Author is not
unaware of this disadvantage, and of the fact that to
some readers many of these notes will be unneces-
sary. But, out of thirty-four years of his work

as a priest, more than twenty were spent mainly
amongst a people—the Church folk of the East
End of London—who are, so far as he is able
to weigh differences, among the noblest of the sons
and daughters of the Church, not only as regards
the much endurance and long patience of their
lives, their sincerity, high-mindedness, and courage,
their freedom from self-indulgence and indolence
on the one hand and from narrowness and stolidity
on the other—characteristics singularly like those
of the Celtic Christians of the pre-mediæval sort
—but also because of their keen and animated interest in all that concerns their Mother in Christ,
and their consecrated zeal for His sake in her service.
But they, and many like them, have not those op-
portunities and facilities of others of their brethren,
represented partly by libraries of their own, or easy
access to those of others, and partly by travel and
literary intercourse; and the Author—having their
needs chiefly in his mind—as they themselves are
nearest to his heart—and the needs, too, of the great
and intelligent body, throughout the whole Church,
of day and Sunday school teachers, and other
Church workers, whose power and influence are

far wider and deeper than some suppose—has thought it right to give full notes rather than only bare references to historical and other authorities.

(2) He has termed his renderings of the reputed Gaelic or Latin poems of St. Columba *Paraphrases* rather than *Translations*, because he is of opinion that no rendering in verse can do justice to an original if it is in any degree a bald and over-exact translation. The full meaning and intention of the writer should of course be given, but in really poetical form, so far as the translator is capable of so rendering the original verses. On the other hand, he is as little in love with a method of paraphrase which is not as close to the original as may fairly be possible in another language.

(3) Those who are not familiar with the old nomenclature which obtained in Columban times should be asked to note that *Scotia* was the name of Ireland, and *Albyn* (or *Albainn*) of Scotland ; and also that where *Scotic* is occasionally used in the notes it is equivalent to Celtic or Irish.

(4) It should be noted—in reference to the fact

that St. Columba and many other abbots of Celtic and later times were priests and not bishops—that to argue from the superiority of abbots in matters of jurisdiction, *quoad civilia*, to a non-recognition in Columban times of the exclusive Apostolical rights of the Episcopate is historically unreasonable.

Columba, during his diaconate, was instructed by a priest, but he was sent to a bishop (Etchen of Clonfad) for ordination. Again, as being only a priest, he refused, during his rule as abbot, to consecrate the Eucharist in the presence of a bishop as his spiritual superior; and moreover, his spiritual descendants in Northumbria—Aidan, Finan, and Colman—were all consecrated.

The only marked difference as regards the Episcopate in the early Celtic Church was that it was not exercised invariably after a territorial or diocesan fashion. The bishops often lived like hermits among the people. In matters of jurisdiction, *quoad civilia*, they were subject to the abbot (in the same way as the Master or Principal of a College at Oxford or Cambridge has collegiate jurisdiction over all the staff of the community, whether any be bishop or no), but, *quoad spiritualia*, the Episcopal rights were unquestioned. As has been well said by the authors of a short *Life of St. Columba* (Mr. W. Muir and the Rev. J. C. Rendell): 'It seemed to be considered that the bishop's sacred power of conferring Holy Orders parted him from ordinary men and made any other duty (except that of manual labour, shared by abbot and all) unworthy of him. Hence the bishop's position was singularly simple, noble, and humble, and was not usually coveted by men who had to lead in affairs. Sanctity was its characteristic then rather than splendour.'

(5) It has seemed advisable to insert after the Preface a short 'Life of St. Columba,' in prose, to facilitate, in some cases at all events, the reading of the poem, and to include some particulars not dealt with in the Cantos.

(6) How great is the debt of this book to Bishop Lightfoot's volume of sermons entitled *Leaders in the Northern Church* (Macmillan) the notes will show. The reader is asked to observe that, after some of the extracts, only the Bishop's name is, for brevity's

sake, given in the notes, with a reference to the page in the edition of 1890.

(7) A few of the miscellaneous poems which close this volume are new. The rest are collected from a variety of Magazines to which the Author has contributed from time to time since the issue of his former volume, *The Knight of Intercession.*

Vestry, All-Hallows'-on-the-Wall,
London Wall, E.C.,
Feast of St. Matthew, Sept. 21, 1897.

A SHORT LIFE OF
ST. COLUMBA

Saint Columba was born at Gartan, in the county of Donegal, Ireland, on December 7th, A.D. 521.

His father, Fedlimidh (or Fedilmith), was a member of the reigning family of Ireland and British Dalriada.

Eithne, his mother, was descended from a King of Leinster.

A vision of Eithne, previous to her son's birth, is described on pp. 45, 46.

He was baptized by a priest named Cruithnechan, who was his foster-father.

His two names (if the tradition as to the double name is true), *Columba* (dove) and *Crimthan* (wolf), are very significant of opposite sides of his character (see pp. 44, 45).

In his early years 'Cille' (*i.e.* 'of the Church' or 'the holy place') was added to his name Columb because of the religious earnestness and Church loyalty which he showed in his boyhood. He passed the years of his early youth at Moville under Bishop Finnian, and was ordained deacon. He studied later on in Leinster under a noted bard named Gemman, and then entered a monastic seminary at Clonard under another St. Finnian; but as this St. Finnian was only a priest, he went for his second ordination to Bishop Etchen of Clonfad.

In 553 he founded the monastery of Durrow, of which Bede makes mention; and, before and after this, a number of other religious houses—said to be more than thirty—owed their origin to his energy and influence. The earliest of these was one in his beloved Derry (see p. 115).

His life up to 561 was one of intense activity and wide usefulness. Then came what may be called the catastrophe of his history, in an act of rebellion and blood-shedding, in the first instance because of his sense of the injustice of a decision of King Diarmid, who refused to enforce the restoration of an illuminated Psalter belonging to Columba and retained by the owner of the book from which it had been copied; and, in the second instance, because of the slaughter by the same king of a youth named Curnan, who had fled to Columba for protection.

Columba, in uttermost indignation, and in the belief that his quarrel was just, after threatening the king, hurried by night from Tara, over the mountains of Tyrconnell, and on his perilous journey he is said to have composed the ' Hymn of Trust,' a paraphrase of which is given at page 116.

After the fashion of those days, he made the matter the subject of a clan quarrel, and eventually a battle was fought in which many men were slain.

According to one account he was, on the instance of the king, excommunicated for bloodguiltiness by a synod of clergy, and only restored on the intercession of St. Brendan. It is said, too, that a priest whom he consulted told him that he was bound, because of his sin, to win to Christ as many pagan souls as he had caused Christian men to be slain in this quarrel.

But Columba, according to one version of the story, knew no peace until another priest named Abban, whom he consulted, told him, after long fasting and prayer, that his ' slain men had the eternal rest.'

Eventually, says a further tradition, under the influence of a hermit named St. Molais of Devenish, he was led to become a voluntary exile from the Erin he so deeply loved, and an evangelist beyond the sight and reach of home and home associations and earthly happiness. Adamnan's words in the Preface to his *Life of St. Columba*, 'Pro Christo peregrinari volens enavigavit,' do not seem so inconsistent with this story as some seem inclined to suppose. Hence, in his forty-second year, his voyage from Erin in a coracle—a wicker boat, sixty feet long, covered with oxhide and thwarted with oakbeams—accompanied (after the manner of the missionary expeditions of those times) by twelve followers or disciples, and their landing on Iona, at what is now called Port-na-Churaich, on Whitsun Eve, May 12, A.D. 563. (See note 3, p. 35.)

So began the practical history of a great Repentance, the 'fruits meet' for which were vast indeed.

Whether the island was conceded to him by his royal kinsman Conall, Lord of Dalriada, or afterwards bestowed upon him by his convert Brude, the Pictish king, is a point of controversy which is not of moment.

His first and chief work was among the heathen Picts of the North of Scotland and of the adjacent islands of the Hebrides; and in the conversion of those who were at first his chief opponents, the Druidic bards. But eventually the evangelising work which he originated in Iona extended not only to the South of Scotland in the resuscitation of the earlier Christian work of St. Ninian, nor only (in his later years) back to Ireland, and in the next century, through St. Aidan and others, on to England from Northumbria throughout the greater part of the Heptarchy; but it reached many parts of the Continent also, in the same way that his Celtic contemporary, St. Columbanus, had evangelised so much of France, Switzerland, and Italy. (See Montalembert, *Monks of the West*, ii. p. 387.) In the words of Bishop Ewing, 'The history of Columba and Iona does not confine itself to the limits of those solitary shores, but, from the necessities of the object with which it is conversant—the evangelisation of Western and Northern Europe—carries us from Iceland in the north to Tarentum in the south, and from the Arctic Seas to the Mediterranean.'—(*Iona*, pp. 1, 2.)

The circumstances of St. Columba's death on June 9, A.D. 597, thirteen hundred years ago this year (1897), are dealt with on pages 197 and 198 of this volume; and those of his burial on pages 69, 70.

The following is the conclusion of the Preface of Abbot Adamnan's great *Life of St. Columba*, written within a hundred years of his death (see Reeves' translation of Adamnan):—

'He was angelic in appearance, graceful in speech, holy in work, with talents of the highest order, and consummate prudence; he lived a soldier of Christ during thirty-four years on an island. He never could spend the space of even one hour without study, or prayer, or writing, or some other holy occupation. So incessantly was he engaged night and day in the unwearied exercise of fasting and watching, that the burden of each of these austerities would seem beyond the power of human endurance. And still in all these he was beloved by all, for a holy joy ever beaming on his face revealed the joy and gladness with which the Holy Spirit filled his inmost soul.'

LAYS OF IONA

AND OTHER POEMS

INTRODUCTORY NOTE TO 'THE SPIRIT OF THE CHURCH FROM IONA'

THE far-reaching work begun by Columba from Iona, and extended in the next century over Northumbria and through the greater part of the Heptarchy by Aidan and his followers, was in the year 664 represented in chief by Colman, Bishop of Lindisfarne.

It was at this time that matters came to a crisis as regards the difference between the Celtic and Roman uses in the calculation of the Easter date and the mode of the tonsure of priests.

By a quibble, as it would seem, the king decided in favour of the Roman view, and Colman resigned his Bishopric.

It is the contention of the following poem that nevertheless the spirit which specially animated the Celtic Church remained, and still abides in that English Church which it did so much to found and to influence.

The following quotations seem to justify the title and the argument of these verses :—

'While all else changes, the *spirit* is unchanged. The simplicity, the self-devotion, the prayerfulness, the burning love for CHRIST which shone forth in those Celtic Missionaries of old must be your spiritual equipment now.'—(BISHOP LIGHTFOOT, *Leaders in the Northern Church*, p. 17.)

'A larger and freer *spirit* (from Iona) must be stamped on the English Church in her infancy never to be obliterated in maturer age.'—(*Ibid.*, p. 41.)

See also Note 3, page 10, from Lecture of the Bishop of Albany, U.S.A.

THE SPIRIT OF THE CHURCH FROM IONA

OR

THE UNION OF THE CELTIC, BRITISH, AND GREGORIAN CHURCHES IN THE ANGLICAN CHURCH

' The Whitby Conference was over: Wilfrid had triumphed: the Paschal Reckoning and the mode of Tonsure were to be Romanised: Colman resigned his Bishopric at Lindisfarne, and retired to Iona: and the Celtic Church was gone.'

(POPULAR STATEMENT.)

SAY ye the Celtic Church is gone,
    As fancies change or friends forget?
The Celtic Church lives on,[1] lives on!
    The Celtic Church is with us yet.

[1] See the notes on preceding page.

Columba's bare Iona lies,
    As he foresaw, a cattle barn ;[1]
Lie stark beneath Northumbrian skies
    The bones of Aidan's Lindisfarne.

Our cradle[2] Isles of West and East—
    They are not as in Aidan's youth ;
What matter ?—if we 'keep the Feast'
    With his 'sincerity and truth.'

Easter is Easter, change who will
    The Calendar that dates the Morn ;
The Priesthood is the Priesthood still,
    Shorn here or there, or all unshorn.

Were Paschal date or Tonsure's plan[3]
    All and be-all of Celtic power?
Gauge ye the spirit of a man
    By regulated hair or hour?

[1] The following is a prose rendering from the Gaelic of a prophecy attributed to Columba :—

    'In Iona of my heart, Iona of my love,
  Instead of monk's voice shall be lowing of kine ;
    But ere the world come to an end
  Shall be Iona as it was.'

The Gaelic and a paraphrase in English verse will be found on p. 114 of this volume.

[2] 'Is not this an opportune time to revert to the cradle of its history and thus link together the last days with the first in the bonds of a natural piety?'—(BISHOP LIGHTFOOT, p. 4.)

[3] See Introductory Note, p. 2.

These things are gone; their graves above
    Iona's living sons may smile;
Columba's force and Aidan's love
    Died not with Colman in his Isle.[1]

Such things may be, such things may fade
    Like tints upon Iona's seas:
Columba's men of war were made
    Of larger elements than these.

These things are gone: let them be gone;
    These be no tests of calm or storm;
It is the spirit that lives on—
    The pure, great heart beneath the form:

The heart unchanged 'neath any skies:[2]
    The giant's heart within the child,
Patient in zeal, in fervour wise,
    The sternly sweet, the gravely mild;

[1] Colman, after his retirement to Iona, died in the island of Innisboffin, off the Irish coast. 'What heart,' writes Montalembert, 'is so cold as not to understand, to sympathise, and to journey with him along the Northumbrian coast and over the Scottish mountains, where, bearing homeward the bones of his father (Aidan), the proud but vanquished spirit returned to his northern mists, and buried in the sacred isle of Iona his defeat and his unconquerable fidelity to the traditions of his race?'

[2] See preliminary notes on p. 2.

That is not gone.　　It lives anew
　　In sons more countless than of eld;
O'er islands wider than they knew
　　It holds the rod of charm it held.

Say not the Celtic Church is gone,
　　Like sunset beam from mountain brow;
The Celtic soul lives on, lives on,
　　The old pure heart is beating now!

Nor say the British Church is gone,[1]
　　As dies some legendary lay;
The British Church lives on, lives on,
　　Saint David's Church is here to-day!

It is the Roman who is gone:
　　I mean not Austin[2]—he is here!
He and his nobles still live on:
　　He and his Gregory still are dear.

[1] 'If any one asks, "Where is the old British Church of what is now England?" the answer is, the old Church is living still. The Bishops of the four Dioceses of Wales rule it still.' . . . 'St. David's probably is the most direct representative of the old British Church of what is now Wales.'—(BISHOP OF STEPNEY, *The Church in These Islands Before Augustine*, pp. 146, 147.)

[2] 'The claims of Rome in this early age were modest indeed compared with her later assumptions. It is an enormous stride from the supremacy of Gregory the Great to the practical despotism claimed by Hildebrand and Innocent III. in the eleventh and succeeding centuries, as it is again a still vaster stride from the latter to the absolute infallibility of Pius IX. in the nineteenth century.'—(BISHOP LIGHTFOOT, p. 51.)

The later Roman—(on whose claim
    Our Austin's Gregory[1] set his ban)—
Who drew the wide Paternal name
    Within his own too meagre span—

The later Roman—with the sword,
    And secular arm, Cæsarean-wise,
Sole, self-elected overlord,
    With hard unspiritual eyes—

'Tis he that from our Isle is gone![2]
    Peace to him on his Tiber shore!
Where'er his claim and he live on,
    His place will know him here no more.

Long time—too long—we knew his spell
    Of mystic toils and sensuous thrills:
The rule that from Iona fell
    Passed to the proud Italian hills.

---

[1] 'Gregory denounces the title of "Universal Bishop" as a proud and pestilent assumption, an act of contempt and wrong to the whole priest-hood, an imitation of Satan, who exalted himself above his fellow-angels, a token of the speedy coming of Antichrist.'—(BISHOP LIGHTFOOT, p. 16.)

[2] Cp. BISHOP LIGHTFOOT, p. 52:—'Through the long ages of Roman domination the English Church was the least enslaved of all the Churches. Her statute-book is a continued protest against this foreign aggression. Her ablest kings were the resolute opponents of Roman usurpation. When the yoke was finally thrown off, though the strong will of the reigning sove-reign was the active agent, yet it was the independent spirit of the clergy and people which rendered the change possible.

'*No more the spell!*'—with seismic throes,[1]
 From agonies as of travail pain,
Once more the purer School arose,
 Iona's doctors taught again.

We learned, 'tis true, to 'organise':[2]
 We learned from Rome her grace and skill,
Art-lore, art-love, a statelier guise,
 A prouder port, a sterner will:

And owe for these fair thanks.[3] Not vain
 Is all that is of beauty's mind;
Let beauty, order, culture, reign
 In all perfection of their kind;

Yet heart is more and soul of love;[4]
 And this in prime we owe not there;—

---

[1] The Reformation.

[2] 'While we are thankful that the foundations of the Northumbrian Church were laid in the simplicity and devotion, the free spirit, the tenderness and love, the apostolic zeal of the missionaries of Iona, we need not shrink from acknowledging that she learnt much from the more complete organisation and the higher culture of which Rome was the schoolmistress.'—(BISHOP LIGHTFOOT, p. 51.) 'The whole (Scotic) system had a rude and homely simplicity. It took no heed of sacred art, was untouched by the influence of the Continental Church atmosphere, and kept its followers aloof from what might be called ecclesiastical civilisation.'—(CANON BRIGHT, *Chapters of Early Church History*, p. 168.)

[3] 'Without the assistance of Rome there could never have been built up in England a great, organised, and cultured Church.'—(WAKEMAN.)

[4] 'Without the help of the saints of Iona that Church would have been

Who says the glory of the dove
    Is in the iris it may bear?

Its glory is the rapture pure
    That makes in peace, not power, its goal :
The Homeward speeding, swift and sure,
    The Heavenward flight of heart and soul.

Columba's this and Aidan's this,
    Oswald's and Hilda's and their kind—
That 'goodliest fellowship'[1] I wis !—
    To them we owe the heart and mind

Which made our *Past* of chill and thrall[2]
    No waste lethargic winter time,
But, though the brumal bond might gall,
    Kept it in true touch with the Prime :—

Which wrought our *Change*,[3] through stormy
    strife
    That brake the dead limbs from the tree,
Back to that Prime of purer life
    And spring-tide carols of the free :—

but a mechanism of bones and flesh wanting the life-giving soul.'—(WAKE-
MAN, *History of Church of England*, p. 26.)

[1] See BISHOP LIGHTFOOT (p. 16), quoting Tennyson's line.

[2] The period under the Papacy.   [3] The Reformation.

Which marks our *Present*,[1] hour by hour,
  With new buds breaking, leaves uncurled,
Beyond the pale of olden power,
  In all the gardens of the world :—

Last : that will make our *Future* rise,[2]
  From seeds of Motherland and Home,
To bear for us 'neath other skies [3]
  Rich fruit in ages yet to come.

Say not Iona's Church is gone,
  As memories die and names decay,
But sing : The British Church lives on
  With Hers and Austin's here to-day.

---

[1] During the sixty years of the reign of Victoria the progress of the Anglican Church is best represented by the extraordinary increase of the Colonial and American as well as of the Home Episcopate.

[2] Predictions of the wonderful future of English-speaking peoples are prophecies too in a measure of the vast extension of the Anglo-Catholic Church.

[3] 'There is a likeness, which proves a lineal descent, between the Church of England of the last three centuries and the Celtic Church of the olden days. . . . Over the seas to us, and over *all* seas, as the Church of England goes with English commerce and English colonisation to the ends of the earth, *it is the old life*, autonomous, independent, needing and knowing no fountain-head but CHRIST, and charged alike with the spirit and the power, the privilege and the responsibility, of bearing the sound of the Gospel in all lands, and its words unto the ends of the world.'—(BISHOP DOANE, of Albany, U.S.A., in Lecture, 'The Celtic Church,' to Church Club of New York, 1889.)

LYRIC OF IONA

PAST, AND TO BE

NOTES TO THE 'LYRIC OF IONA'

[1] *Port-na-Churaich* (the Haven of the Coracle) is at the south-west end of the island. Here St. Columba landed with his twelve followers on the eve of Whitsunday, May 12, A.D. 563, and having ascended to the point near it, now called 'Cairn cul ri Erin' (or 'Cairn of Farewell to Ireland'), and seeing that his native land was not visible (as it had been from Colonsay, the island on which he first landed), he decided to make Iona the cradle of his Mission. It is in this bay that the brilliantly coloured stones, white and porphyry-coloured and (most beautiful of all) translucent green serpentine and the reddest felspar, are found.

[2] *Eala* is the grassy mound above 'Martyr's Bay' on which the bodies brought by the galleys from distant places for burial in the Reilig Oran were laid, after disembarkation, previously to their passage along the 'Street of the Dead' to the Reilig. The word is sometimes derived from the Gaelic for a *swan*. The real derivation is from *calatrom*, a *bier*.

[3] *The Reilig Oran* (or Odhrain) on the east side of the island, near the Sound which separates Iona from Mull, is the famous place of sepulture near St. Oran's Chapel. The position of the ruin of this chapel is considered the most probable site of the church in which Columba worshipped. In the Reilig Oran, the most hallowed burial-place in Scotland, lie buried sixty-one kings—forty-eight of Scotland, eight of Norway, four of Ireland, and one of France, besides many bishops, abbots, priests, and chieftains. (See later note, p. 63.)

[4] 'Close beyond the Reilig Odhrain, a little to the north-east, there is a natural hillock of rock, but covered on most sides by turf, which is perhaps the most interesting spot upon Iona. From its isolated position—from its close proximity to St. Odhrain's Chapel, and to the ancient place of sepulture . . . from the splendid view it commands over the sacred objects close at hand, over the sloping fields, the Sound, the opposite coast, and the distant mountains—this knoll must have been a favourite resort of all the generations of men who lived and worshipped on Iona. Tradition, too, has faithfully preserved in its Gaelic name the identity of the spot. It is called the "Torr-Abb," or the "Abbot's Knoll." I cannot doubt that it is "the little hill" respecting which Adamnan gives perhaps the most remarkable anecdote in his account of Columba's life. On the last day of that life, Columba, we are told, being now very infirm, ascended a "little hill" (Monticellulum) . . . and lifting up both his hands, he blessed his now long-adopted home, and pronounced this prophecy of its fame: "Unto this place, albeit so small and poor, great homage shall yet be paid, not only by the Kings and people of the Scots, but by the rulers of barbarous and distant nations, with their people also. In great veneration, too, shall it be held by the holy men of other Churches."'—(DUKE OF ARGYLL'S *Iona*, p. 89, etc.)

Lyric of Iona: Past, and To Be.

I

A HERMIT spirit holds the isle ;
    Ever, by night, by day,
His eyes are in its matin smile,
    And in its vesper ray ;
But most he loves the haunted ground
        From Columb's bay[1]
        To Eala's mound,[2]
And where St. Oran's dead sleep by the rolling
    Sound.[3]

II

A spirit he of hope and love,
    Free as the wind and wave,
Nor more is he as brooding dove,
    Than as a prophet brave ;
An he must mourn, 'tis not with moan,
        For each rough grave,
        Each ruin lone,
Is in his far-off look a new foundation-stone.

III

He holds for all the Isle in spell
 Who from Torr Abb[4] can hear
The old immortal oracle
 Still wed the far and near:
There ever, for the impassioned eye
  And wistful ear,
  He summons nigh
The deeds that live like song, the Creeds that
 cannot die.

IV

Haunt me, sweet spirit of the Isle!
 Thou tender soul and strong!
From Duni's steep to yon grey pile,
 And each wild strand along,
Back to the amethystine shore,
  Thine undersong
  Be evermore
Love's brooding on the wind, Hope's music in
 the roar.

CANTO THE FIRST

Introduction

I

If, pilgrim-poet, thou would'st soothe thine eyes
   Long time aweary of thy prison walls,
Seek not the ever-azure seas and skies
   Where nought of change upon thy vision falls,
   Where fairest scene no fairer deed recalls;
Though there tired head and languid limb may rest,
   Thy heart, like hungry wight in barren halls,
Or spirit fair displumed and dispossessed,
Will roam the lovely land unsated and unblest.

II

Go, rather, where, as on Iona's shore,
   Soft vales, or breeze-impassioned pines, or streams
That woo the summer, or, from mountains frore,
   Roll winter, *are not*—but a silence seems
   The reverent guardian of a land of dreams:

Silence all deepened by th' Atlantic surge,
  And loud or crooning winds and seafowl screams—
Silence that is a memory, not a dirge;
Dreams from whose pregnant depths right-royal
  forms emerge.

III

Rapt silence: like a memory in a song
  So sacred it is sung beneath the breath,
Wherein a host of saints and heroes throng,
  Yet never fear or folly entereth
  With alien step or strident note; but Death
Stands starry-crowned, as Hope, and like a friend
  Greets each mute presence there as one who saith :
'Your old highway of triumph still ye wend;
Not yours, ye Great, but mine, mine is the gloom
  and End!'

IV

Dreams of no heights or depths of spectral air :—
  No idle fancy's unsubstantial food
Feeble for use, albeit to vision fair—
  But dreams that nerve the heart, and fire the
    blood,
  And brace the laggard limbs of purpose crude,

With longings for ripe action—dreams that breed
   Stern impulses of such a fortitude
As dares, amid a world of pomp and greed,
To live that life of use which must be life of deed.

V

But one, nor greatest, of a hundred Isles [1]
   'Tis first in fame, if deepest in the gloom ;
Authentic still above her ghostly piles
   A living Voice denies the seeming doom,
   And still the stately Crosses o'er her tomb—[2]
To faithful hearts in every land a lure—
   The grey sepulchral solitudes illume ;
Long as the Church lives and its Creeds endure,
Shall be their lonely light a Christian cynosure.

[1] Sir Donald Munro, in his *Description of the Western Isles, called the Hebrides* (1549), gives the names of two hundred and nine islands.

[2] The popular tradition is that there were more than three hundred crosses on Iona before their general destruction was ordered by the Presbyterian Synod.

The crosses here specially alluded to are those well known by the names of (1) *Maclean's Cross*, in the Street of the Dead, a monolith about eleven feet high, hewn out of mica schist, said to have been erected on the spot where St. Columba sat to rest on the afternoon before he died : and is probably therefore the oldest Christian monument in Britain ; and (2) *St. Martin's Cross*, a solid column of hard rock, fourteen feet high, in the grounds of the Cathedral ruins. Both are probably of much more ancient date than that of the ruins, and are therefore to be associated with the Celtic not the Cluniac monks.

VI

Here was new-born to GOD the northern West.[1]

   Here for the West 'gan beat that pastoral heart,

A child's heart yet a giant's, in the breast

   Of simple men, that with no other art

   Or wile, save Love's, could front each devil's dart

Of fear, or worse self-favour, with the pride

   In Cause or Captain where self played no part—

That warrior-heart unchecked—as ocean's tide

Resistless, swift or slow, o'er rock or dune can ride.

VII

Not for thine earthly beauty dearest thou,

   Iona, of the Isles.   Chief beauty stands

By heart and life, by unforgotten vow,

   By acted penitence, by holy hands

   Of prayer and service at the dear demands

Of Him Who adds to 'I forgive thee' 'Go!'[2]

   Then in the oblation of love-conquered lands,

Of peace and gladness for revenge and woe,

Of brethren of one heart for yon vindictive foe.

---

[1] An old title of Iona, 'The Western Morning Star,' was given to it in allusion to the conversion of Pictland by St. Columba and his monks.

[2] There is a close analogy between the question of the penitent Saul of Tarsus, 'LORD, what wilt Thou have me to do?' and his obedience to the bidding that he should go to the Gentiles, with its results, and Columba's 'fruits meet for repentance' brought forth after absolution had followed on his acknowledged transgression.

CANTO THE FIRST

The Island

I

Yet thou art beautiful,[1] above, below,
  Wild or serene; in rock, in heav'n, in wave.
Now all the immense Atlantic, in its flow
  Of furious storm thy warder headlands brave;
  Now not more still and holy is a grave
That flowers look down to and the tender skies,
  And water-kisses as for worship lave;
While breezes soft as slumber fall and rise,
And rise and fall again in reverential sighs.

---

[1] 'There are not many places in the world where those three great voices—"each a mighty voice"—the sky, the sea, the mountains—can be heard sounding in finer harmony than round Columba's Isle.'—(DUKE OF ARGYLL.)

II

Hues of Iona's waters and her heaven ! [1]
When winds are up or when they sink to rest,
To what fair daughter of the seas is given
To be with more variety invest?
Scarce may the Indian islands of the West
With eyes of light intenser plead with fame
To be for sure the Islands of the Blest.
O eyes of morn, O sunset eyes aflame,
And ye translucent floods, ye seal her sovereign
claim !

III

O not forlorn, though Solitude be queen !
As the Divine Election, if it chose
A spot so faint in all the vast Terrene,[2]
Would choose it where the freest sea-wind blows

---

[1] 'It is true that the climate of the Hebrides is a wet one. Hence the wonderful beauty of the skies. "Cloudland, gorgeous cloudland," is a truthful exclamation of the poet. For nowhere is the face of heaven more various in expression than along that line of coast where the vapours of the Atlantic are first caught by the Highland hills. . . . It is true the colouring is darker, but it is also deeper, richer—more intense. Nothing can exceed its splendour. And so of the sea : its aspects around Iona are singularly various and beautiful.'—(DUKE OF ARGYLL, *Iona*, pp. 69-71.)

[2] Iona is in length not more than three miles and less than a mile and a half in breadth. In a map of Europe it is of course only represented by a nameless dot.

With tales of the great deep;[1] where Beauty glows
I' th' arms of ocean sunsets, or in light
  Of changeful hues that ever interpose
"Twixt shade and shine from morn to midday height :
Or broods, like love in heaven, thro' the long norland
    night.

IV

Dark based, dark lined, thy rocks are ashen grey,
  Stark as a skeleton : as they had been,
In dateless ages of the far-away,
  The monstrous relics of some astral queen
  Doomed and flung down as on a grave obscene,
Lashed by the spray, mocked by the gales a while,
  Till—lo, came Pity, clad in tenderest green,[2]
Where winds and waves forbade her not, to smile,
And from these bones of death to form the living
    Isle.

[1] On the western side of the island there is 'nothing to break the fetch of the ocean from the shores of the New World.'

[2] 'It is true Iona is a rocky island, the bones protruding at frequent intervals through the skin of turf. Even there, however, Columba must have seen that the pasture was close and good ; and not far from the spot on which he first swept the southern sky, he must have found that the heathy and rocky hills subsided into a lower tract, green with that delicious turf which, full of thyme and wild clovers, gathers upon soils of shelly sand.'—(DUKE OF ARGYLL.)

V

And most she bade the soft green grasses grow

   On one fair mound that fronts th' Atlantic main—[1]

Whose roar, as of the ages, flings below—

   As she would clothe it thus, in meek disdain

Of salt sea wrath.—Mark it by Machar's plain,

Where spread she soil for many a fruitful field,

   A stiller sea to roll in golden grain ;—

'Tis hight, 'The Angels' Hill.' There Columb kneeled,

And o'er him spirits of grace in choral blessing

     wheeled.

VI

Thus did she robe that ruin with her spring.

   Here with tall grasses : there with elfin lawn :

To blanched crushed homes of life[2] made mosses cling

   As green as hope, or golden as the dawn :

---

[1] 'There is a story of one of his monks having followed him secretly to the round grassy hill near the western shore of the island, looking over the Atlantic, and beheld him surrounded with white-robed companies of Angels who stood around him as he prayed. This hill is still called the Angels' Hill in Iona in the language St. Columba spoke.'—(*Early Missions*, etc., Mrs. RUNDLE CHARLES, S.P.C.K., p. 146.) This little hill is the *colliculus angelorum* of Adamnan.

[2] The 'silver sand' at the north and east of the island, and in other parts of it, is composed of the pulverised shells of an infinity of small land snails. Here and there the grasses and clovers flourish on it.

And many a modest flower, from sight withdrawn,
Set in the heath and fern.   Yet there and here
  Are rocks all robe, save lichen, have forgone ;
Some spire the knolls, some through the mosses peer :
Some huge, might scare a maid or charm a moun-
    taineer.

VII

One like a crouching lion is on guard :
  One like an old-world monster lies asleep :
Here a tall sentinel keeps rigid ward
  Fronting a weird and wave-worn castle keep :
  One sphinx-like gazes calmly o'er the deep :
While 'twixt the mightier masses wide and far
  Vast fragments lie alone in rugged heap—
Her bones who lost the Queendom of a star !—
Or missiles hurled from heaven in some Titanic war !

VIII

There mark yon solan hovering o'er the sound ;
  Like a doomed life, it plunges in the wave :
Silverly leaps the spray in sudden bound !
  Then sudden sinks—like tears upon a grave

When piteous sorrow sighs that none can save,
And green seas like green grasses hide beneath
　Their rippling pall the beautiful and brave—
Ah ! for a moment dost thou hold thy breath
To see the great bird spring out from its seeming
　　death ?

IX

Like its own ghost it crowns its former tomb :
　Refreshed and fed by seeming loss it soars :
So springs a spirit from the fancied doom
　Of some deep purpose : depth to height restores
　Its troth-trust :—so the Patriarch of these shores
Sprang from his exile into use and fame.
　He prays i' the depth who last i' the height adores :
Who loses life itself in toil or shame
Finds more than that he lost and wins the elect new
　　name.

X

Hast marked yon scattered rocks red-veined and vast,[1]
　Mull's children alien here?　Alone they lie,
As each had been some Titan's wrathful cast
　From the Great Isle in times too long gone by

[1] Iona is entirely composed, says the Duke of Argyll, of strata which he

For record!   Canst not hear the sullen cry
Of jealous wrath with each red bolt impelled,
Wrath that the less the greater should outvie?'—
No Titan's bolts are these, but ice-drift held
In some frore torrent's grasp that vexed the shores
    of eld!

XI

Yet have I caught thy fancy, pilgrim!   Lo,
    Thine agèd Isle that is more great by age,
First daughter of the mystic long ago,
    Did reck so lightly of yon Titan's rage
    Who dared profane her lonely hermitage,
And thinking scorn of childish blow for blow,
    Moved only to lift up one bolt for gage
On yon three mocking fingers to her foe,
And all these myriad years disdained to let it go.

believes to belong to the oldest sedimentary rock yet known as existing in the world—the Laurentian gneiss. Mull, on the contrary, is of red granite. But Mull strangely has its representatives in Iona in several huge masses of its granite brought over by ice in the glacial period : notably a gigantic boulder of about two hundred tons to the north of the Cathedral, and a smaller one, but of vast weight, beyond Martyr's Bay. This boulder is, as if contemptuously (see Stanza XI.), balanced on small points of the harder and more ancient rock of Iona.

XII

Peace to these idle fancies !   'Tis enough
    That children shelter 'neath it in the shade,
Or when the winds on rainy seas are rough,
    Or the last games on the white sand are played.
    Come with more human fancies to mine aid !
Hard by is Eala's holy mound of death,
    And Martyr's Bay.   No thought may here invade
Save love's or fear's.   Here slowly entereth
Reverence with far-off mien and musings 'neath her
    breath.

XIII

A thousand years, from lands the far away,
    Or from familiar clans on isles anear,
To sleep till these earth-shadows flee at day,
    They brought their greatest and their saintliest
    here ;[1]

---

[1] ' Nor can we fail to remember, with the Reilig Odhrain at our feet, how often the beautiful galleys of that olden time came up the Sound laden with the Dead—"their dark freight a vanished life." . . . The tombstones of the Reilig represent the lasting reverence which Columba's name has inspired during so many generations, and the desire of a long succession of kings and chiefs to be buried in the soil he trod.'—(DUKE OF ARGYLL, pp. 97, 98. See also note on p. 63.) The following extract from Adamnan's *Life of St. Columba* (Book III. ch. xxiv.) tells us of this usage: ' *Honeste ternis diebus et totidem noctibus honorabiles rite explentur exequiæ,*' ' His obsequies were celebrated with all due honour and reverence for three days and as many nights.'

O'er the white sands upborne the sacred bier
Sank to first rest on Eala's breast-like mound;
　　Then priest's low prayer and choral chanting clear,
Like incense of the spring from April ground,
Mingled with break of wave and wind that swept the
　　Sound.

XIV

Three days, three nights that vigil's swell and fall
　　Of song and prayer the waiting galleys heard;
Death-still they joined the stately funeral,
　　Slow-rocking on the Bay.　The wild sea-bird,
　　As stayed by spell, with wings that only stirred
In rhythmic wise, wraith-like, did overhang;
　　Then at the close—the last absolving word—
Began the sad slow tread and armoured clang:
And still the surges plunged and still the sea-wind
　　sang.

XV

Climb, with the morn, yon slópes about Duni;[1]
　　Look from the height on all St. Columb saw,

---

[1] Duni, or Dunii, is the small mountain of Iona, 330 feet high. The view
from it on a clear day is unsurpassable in beauty and interest. To the
south are the Paps of Jura, to the north in the near distance the natural
Cathedral of Staffa, in the far distance the Cuchulin mountains of Skye,
and all are visible though the distance between Jura and Skye is ninety-
six miles. To the south-west is the vast Atlantic stretching out to the

On nature all unchanged.[1]   Less wilt thou see
  On many a mightier mountain—less for awe,
  Or the delight of free-far gaze ; no flaw
Or bar on amplest vision lets thee now !
  Thine eye to all the winds makes its own law,
Leagues long three-score the seas its range allow,
From southern Jura's breasts to Coolin's awful brow.

XVI

The Isles, three-score, like monsters of the deep,
  From farthest Islay on to frowning Skye,
Rest on the dark-blue waters as in sleep,
  Or as huge kine on sea-like prairies lie,
  Ruminant at the noon.   A soft-breathed sigh
O' the mother of many moods now croons along
  From cove to scaur—a kiss, a lullaby
O' the wind, who may ere night, a fury strong,
Scream against reef and cliff her threats of scathe
  and wrong.

New World; eastward are Mull and its mountains ; and below and between, the most sacred part of the island is in clear view beside the Sound.
  [1] 'When we look on Iona, or when we range the wide horizon visible
from its shores, we are tracing the very outlines which Columba's eye has
often traced, we follow the same winding coasts, the same stormy headlands, the same sheltered creeks, the same archipelago of curious islands,
and the same treacherous reefs by which Columba has often sailed. . . .
All the great aspects of nature upon and around Iona must be the same
as they were thirteen hundred years ago.'—(DUKE OF ARGYLL.)

XVII

But now—the centre of a hundred miles,
  Thou feel'st no breath but that of the sea balm
That braces while it soothes.   The waves, the isles,
  Lie like a vision of peace in stately calm—
  Less stately were the coco and the palm
Than yon rock piles !   Below, the Minster tower
  Is silence eloquent—a lofty Psalm—
That lifts thee ' to the Timeless from the Hour':
On all this earthly show GOD's seal of heavenly power.

XVIII

Most beauteous scene ! thrice hallowed by one Hand :
  Here by His Cross-sign on His holiest Isle :
There by His mightiest Church on sea or land,
  Great Staffa's fane—the lone stupendous pile
  Whose far-encircling Close, and long-drawn Aisle,
And Organ—is the sea ! and last, above,
  The Over-soul in sight, the FATHER's smile,
The Dome where broods in light th' Eternal DOVE—
O'er-watching tenderness, o'er-arching visible love.

XIX

Rise : thou hast drunk thy fill of this delight.
    But soon thy beaker shall be brimmed again
With other wine o' the Isle in sound and sight.
    Change stirs in the still air, and from the main
    Westward a warning moans, like his whom pain
Has waked from quiet sleep.   Westward go down,
    As he from Carmel sped before the rain,
Past Machar's fringe of mosses golden brown,
Where by the Spectral Cave the great Rock-warders
       frown.[1]

XX

See how the storm rides up !   This western shore
    Awaits the inset of its noon-day tide
As of a horde of foes.   The water-roar,
    The fierce wind-blare, herald the hosts allied
    'Gainst yon rock-chiefs set there in sombre pride,
Like scarred grey-headed warriors, sternly grave,
    Who all the years all onsets have defied.

---

[1] This cave, called the Spouting Cave, is one of several among the rugged cliffs on the south-west part of the island. When the wind is high and the waves large, the water, in a columnar form, spouts to the height of about two hundred feet, descending like a cataract.—(See DR. GORDON's *Iona*, p. 51.)

See how they tear the cartel ocean gave !
Leap, thou torn surge, and fall—weird column of
    the cave !

XXI

'Tis eve, and ebb of tide : the winds are falling,
    An army sullen in retreat; the seas
Rage on like veterans careless of the calling
    To end a noble strife in craven ease.
    Yet must they fall too ; scarcely now a breeze
Sighs its despair.   Yet fails there not a sign
    Of martial end in fitting obsequies ;
A sunset glory makes their waters wine :
Surges and rocks alike its beams incarnadine.

XXII

Now midnight sleeps: but murmurs while she dreams
    As still awake to love.   The waters sleep,
Save where the autumn queen her wealth of beams
    Pours in such royal largesse that the deep,
    Else dark and silent, seems to start and leap
With myriad elfin hands to grasp the boon,
    And myriad elfin eyes that wake and peep

In merry wise, to find again so soon
That sweet light lately lost i' the maelstrom of the
　　noon.

XXIII

' Immense the conversation of the sea,'
　　One says who loves the Isle.[1]　In power or rest :
In sound or voiceful silence : bound or free :
　　Moon-drawn and subject, or as one possessed
　　With more of might and passion, or of zest
For dance and laughter, than all else God-wrought ;
　　Now eagle-pinioned, *now* upon its nest
Creation's dove of sad or solemn thought :—
Where more than round these shores with various
　　beauty fraught ?

[1] THE DUKE OF ARGYLL, *Iona*, p. 68.

A Lay of Port-na-Churaich

I

Rock and roar,
Wind and wave, of a west-rolling sea,
       Of a sunset of sea:
The deep slope of a diamond shore,[1]
       A mosaic of shore:
And a moss-hidden skeleton lea,
       Lying inward afar
From sea-gates of precipitous scaur:—
Like their spell was none other to me,
       Is none other to me!

II

Face and form,
Port and power, of a ruler of men
       Of a Saul among men:[2]
Voice like song at the heart of a storm,
       A deep organ of storm:

C

Kingly eye as an eagle's in ken,
Yet an angel might own
Looking love by the steps of the Throne;
Their old glamour is now as was then :
Even now as was then !

III

Long ago?
And ye hear but the roll of the wind,
Of the wave and the wind,
But the ebb, or the plunge of the flow,
Sough of ebb, thunder-flow?
And ye see not these wraiths of the mind?
And that old Pentecost [3]
Is a thing of the Far-away lost?
And I sing to the deaf and the blind,
Spirit-deaf, spirit-blind?

IV

Ah, no, no !
By the winds would a challenge be hurled,
From the West [4] would be hurled;
By the seas, by their many-hued Bow,
By their opaline Bow—

That the Banner of Love is unfurled

Over space without bound :

That this glamour of vision and sound

Has won through the gates of the world,

Of yon world and your world !

---

[1] See note on page 12.

[2] The following is translated from the Latin of Adamnan's *Life of S. Columba* (Book I. ch. i.):—

' King Oswald, after pitching his camp in readiness for the battle, was sleeping one day in his tent, and he saw St. Columba in a vision beaming with angelic brightness, and of a figure so majestic that his head seemed to touch the clouds.'

(Also see note on page 57 of this volume.)

[3] Those who have access to Mrs. Rundle Charles' *Tria juncta in Uno : Early Christian Missions in Scotland*, S.P.C.K., would do well to read the admirable description of Eve of Whitsunday and the next days' Festival on May 12, 13, A.D. 563 (pages 113-117).

[4] The expanse of sea westward from Port-na-Churaich is unbroken to that New World, the present Christian obedience of which is so largely due in its Anglo-Saxon population to the Missionary work originated in Iona, and where the Episcopal Succession was first received through the Catholic Church of Scotland.

CANTO THE SECOND

The Names of the Island

I

Truth and true love, in one, to their elect
   Have many voices.   Stately first the tone
And unimpassioned, when their mood's respect
   Looks far away; but, last, when they have grown
   By nearness tender-hearted, and have known
The thrills of contact, they with softer grace
   And more of music sweetly name their own,
Like souls love-rapt from common Time and Place
Who wander hand in hand, or murmur face to face.

II

'Isle of the Druids'[1] wast thou named of yore;
   Ere from the Orient to thine Occident
Brake the new Light—ere, hallowing thy shore,
   Stood Columb and his Twelve, and o'er thee bent

---

[1] Whatever may be said against some of their practices and their comparative ignorance, the Druids should have the credit due to them of having reached and encouraged a civilisation generally in advance of their time.

New Pentecostal skies.   More excellent
Than that high [1] path thy Druid fathers trod
    Emmanuel's way !   The Great Bard to thee sent
Sang the new Song, bare the true 'Fire of God'!
So fell before His Sign the old Druidic Rod.

III

Thou wert '*Iouan Isle*' [2] of Adamnan—
    Columba's son and leal Evangelist,
Who limned so well the marvel of the man
    That his great form through the millennial mist
    Shows   clear   as   'gainst   clear   sky   o'er   waters
        whist ;
'*Ishona*' [3] hight, as Gaelic legends tell,
    The Island ever 'Holy' to The CHRIST :
And '*Icolmkill*,' [4] the sea-girt citadel
Of   Columb   of   the   Church,   or   Columb   of   the
        Cell.

[1] See note on preceding page.

[2] *Ioua Insula* is the invariable form of name in all ancient MSS. of Adamnan (see REEVES' *Life of Columba*, pp. cxxviii.-cxxx.).

[3] *Ishona* : from the two Gaelic words for Holy Island.   It is a mistake to derive Iona from this name.

[4] *Icolmkill*: otherwise *Icolumkill* or *Icolmcille* : in each case meaning 'The Island of Columb of the Church' or 'of the holy place.'

IV

By one thou art imperially alone;
  '*H Y*'[1] by the eld yclept, as if it knew—
Knew, yet not knew—that there could be but one,
    One 'Island' only in the reverent view
    Of Christian eyes—one by election true
Of the Divine fore-knowledge—one by grace
    Set o'er the mightiest to claim thy due,
Though 'least,' like her of Ephratah,[2] in space,
Mother-in-God to be of a most royal race.

V

A second Bethlehem, second Nazareth,
    So mean of style, or title, or repute :
Yet so life-gifted by the Lord of Death
    To be the 'House of Bread,' where David's root,
    The stately Tree of Life, should spring and shoot,
And for far nations of the saved should bear
    Its healing leaves and amaranthine fruit,
Albeit in such dry ground and desert air,
Eternal Solitude seemed fittest sovereign there.

---

[1] *Hy*, or *I*, simply means Island.
[2] Micah v. 2

VI

'*Iona*' last.   There 's music in thy name,
    Iona! and, to souls with ears to hear,
True music and sweet meaning are the same,
    Filling with dulcet thought the grateful ear—
    Fair poesie to all singing is so near!—
Iona, dear Iona, evermore,
    Let flout that name who will with test austere,
May the sweet error[1] on th' enchanted shore
Rule in thy rainbow heaven, swell in thine ocean's
    roar.

[1] There can be little doubt that this musical name, now, we hope, never to be changed, came originally from the error, accidental or other, of the substitution of *n* for *u*. No scholar seems to agree with Colgan, who, being impressed with the notion, 'mendose Ioua pro Iona,' printed Iona in all the shorter lives of his Collection, as also in his abridgment of O'Donnell, although the reading was probably different in the originals.—(REEVES, cxxix.)

Hymn of Iona and the Isles

'Son of man, can these bones live?'—Ez. xxxvii. 3.

I

Bleak o'er the Isle the bones of death
　To all the winds lie bare:
Not yet has blown the new wind's breath,
　No throb of life is there:
The sapphire sky, the rainbow sea
Alone forecast the things to be.

III

The cormorant's [1] and the raven's wing
　Sweep over surge and shore;
As 'gainst a dead or dying thing
　The sullen breakers roar:
LORD GOD of life, the Isle is Thine,
O bid Thy dead arise and shine!

---

[1] The cormorant is one of the most familiar birds of the Hebrides; and
Albyn (Scotland) was known specially as the ' Land of the Raven.'

III

Jesus, Iona waits Thy will!
  Till light upon her smiles;
Waits, too, in silence dark and chill
  The multitude[1] of Isles:
Till she may wake their choral throng
To join her own adoring song.

IV

Hark, o'er the waters far away
  Is heard the CHRIST's command!
See now on yonder gleaming Bay
  A new Ezekiel stand:
Great seer, thy Master's message give,
Bid these dry bones awake and live!

V

From Whitsun[2] to Ascension morn,
  As each year lives and dies,
'Gainst Pagan[3] threat and poet scorn
  Saint Columb prophesies:

---

[1] See note on page 17.　　　　[2] See Note 3 on page 35.
[3] The chief early opponents of the Celtic Mission were the Pictish Pagans and the Druidic Bards.

See from the wide West's charnel sod
A white-robed army lives to GOD.

VI

O FATHER, Thine eternal choice,
   O SON, Thy love divine,
O HOLY GHOST, Thy quickening voice,
   Made every isle a shrine !
Their lauds of love, O ONE IN THREE,
Iona's children lift to Thee.

Amen.

CANTO THE THIRD

Columba: his Birth, Names, Early Years

I

Of ancient line and royal [1] wast thou born,
  Thou king of men.　Two crowns in promise throwing
    throwing
Their glow upon thy cradle at the morn
    Foretold the day.　Yet men stood by unknowing
    What Will ordained, or whose the Hand bestowing
Thy chrism and regalia.　Who was 'ware
  The things eternal in that light were glowing?
Not Donegal nor Leinster crowned thee there!
Thee for Anointed King a hundred realms must
    share.

II

'Columba' [2] named.　Willed the eternal Dove
  To be in His own sign thus honoured most,

---

[1] His father, Feidlimbh, was of the royal blood of Donegal; his mother, Eithne, of that of Leinster.

[2] Columba, in Latin, a Dove.　It may be noted here that because the word Iona in Hebrew signifies Dove, some have therefore fancied that

Since for new miracle of power and love,
   Wrought for the heavy-laden or the lost,
   Renewal blest of primal Pentecost,
He sealed thee such great mission to fulfil—
   Thee and thy twelve from one small Island's post—
As twelve from one small room on Zion's Hill
Sped with the CHRIST to win the whole wide world
     from ill.

III

Yet 'Crimthan'[1] too.   Didst suck the breast of
   kings
That blood of warriors rather than the stream
Of gentle mother's milk—(what time she sings
   Lullaby to her babe)—a while would seem
   Flood of thy veins, and th' impassioned gleam,
Men call 'the light of battle,' in thine eyes
   Would steel that winning smile, or break the dream
Of that exalted soul whose phantasies[2]
Rapt commune loved to hold with spirit-peopled
   skies ?

this fact was the origin of that name for the Island. This, no doubt, is not correct. But the Latin word easily lends itself to a Pentecostal suggestion.

[1] *Crimthan*, that is *Wolf.* It would appear that both names were given him at the same time, before or at his baptism.

[2] From before St. Columba's birth, and afterwards from his boyhood

IV

Nay: mother's son was he, that lordly Celt;
   Eithne, thy hands were not more woman-smooth
For churl or child! his clear grey eyes could melt
   At every call of tenderness or ruth
With love like thine :—like thine, for age or youth,
In all extreme of need, th' impulsive heart,
   As pity were its sovran law in sooth,
Beat with full pulse, spent each most patient art
Sorrow's deep wound to heal or sin's more venomed
    smart.

V

Eithne! to mother's hope how proudly bright—
   To mother's memory, in its patience strong,
How blest—the dream [1] of that prophetic night,
   That stately Presence from th' angelic throng,

on throughout his life, many instances are characteristically given by Adamnan, on a variety of testimony, of angelic visitations and manifestations in his behalf. (See Book III. on the Visions of Angels.)

[1] The following is a shortened translation from the Latin of Adamnan's account of Eithne's vision :—

' Between his conception and his birth, an angel of the Lord appeared to his mother in dreams, bringing to her a robe of extraordinary beauty, in which the most beautiful colours, as of all the flowers, seemed to be portrayed. After a short time he took it out of her hands, and spreading it out let it fly through the air. But she being sad at the loss of it, said : "Why dost thou take this so lovely robe from me so soon?" He replied :

The robe of myriad hues—for which did long
Thy woman's eye—rapt, ere possessed, away,
  Yet still possessed, like a remembered song,
Stored for delight—that infinite array
Of flowers thick-strewn as stars, and beauteous as
    the day.

VI

'Stored for delight,' for more than won thine eye,
  For noble promise to thy soul.   It sped
Far o'er the plains, out to the northern sky,
  Past mount and forest ever more dispread,
  Enfolding all with beauty.   Then he said:
'Rather give thanks: ere long to thee shall come
  A prophet-son who, in his Master's stead,
  Shall lead from wastes where lost sheep sadly roam
Souls countless as these flowers, safe to their
    Heavenly Home.'

" Because this robe is of such exceeding honour that thou canst not longer
retain it."   Then she saw the robe recede in flight and expand until its
width exceeded the plains, the mountains, and the forests.   Then she heard
these words: " Woman, grieve not, for thou shalt bring forth a son of so
beautiful a character, that he shall be reckoned as one of the prophets of
God, and hath been predestined by God to be the leader of countless souls
to the heavenly country." '   (Book III. chap. ii.)

VII

Thus, as upon his LORD's in Holy Land,
    Upon his birth an angel blessing fell,
Blessing his after-growth.   We see him stand,
    Fulfilment meet for such an oracle,
    Himself angelic,—seraph-tongued to tell
His Master's message, and with Stephen's face
    Twice holy, stern and tender, like a spell,
Now a strong warrior's, now a woman's, grace,
The surest to o'erthrow, the readiest to embrace.

Farewell:
A Song of Love and Duty

(FOR MUSIC)

I

Farewell—so soon, so late—Farewell, Farewell:
So soon, with chirp of dawn, the Passing Bell:
      Farewell, Farewell.

So late: it lingers, throbbing down the wind:
It thrills, with touch of death, thro' heart and
    mind:
      Farewell, Farewell.

It lives to haunt the glow and heat of day:
It dies not when the eve is cold and grey:
      Farewell, Farewell.

The lone night-watchers hear the toll forlorn,
Till once again it antedates the morn:
      Farewell, Farewell.

II

Yet 'neath and o'er Farewell, or soon or late,
A spirit moves—secure of time and fate :
        Lord of Farewell.

Toll, toll Farewell, from the drear sunrise on,
Yet shall not Will be quenched, nor Work fore-
    gone
        Beneath Farewell.

Till at some dawn far off, with glad surprise
To all Farewell itself out of new skies
        Is pealed Farewell.

CANTO THE FOURTH

Columba: Transgression, Repentance, and Self-Exile

I

Bright was the sunrise, bright the morning sky
    That glowed and deepened as the splendid flower
Brake from the bud of boyhood, towering high
    Over its garden fellows.   Such a power
    Was in him linked with sweetness and the dower
Of grace, the dew of Hermon, on his soul,
    Few might foresee and fear the cloudlet lower
That gloomed erelong the clear meridian pole,
Big with devouring flame and voiced with thunder
    roll.

II

Woe worth it that a Spring of youth so rare,
    Summer of fullest flower of bent and aim,
And Autumn that such early fruitage bare—
    Fruitage of love that fairer is than fame,

And with a holier halo orbed his name—
That such a life should seem to lose its crown ;
  Albeit on righteous anger rests no shame,
Albeit on crime e'en Love herself may frown,
Yet she on such stern mood lets not the sun go
  down.

III

He let the sun go down upon his wrath,
  And gave his enemy place—and it was night.
False lures of passion played about his path :—
  How great the darkness, when the dark seems
    light !
  The anger born of Sorrow and of Right
Was fed by vengeful fury till it grew
  A changeling monster of disease and blight ;
He that was Abel stands a Cain to view,
Whom for fair foe or friend nor man nor angel knew.

IV

So on that Abel fell the curse of Cain,
  The Church her 'Columb of the Church' of yore
In Crimthan of the slaughter seeks in vain ;
  The aureole that ringed his brows before

Is all out-blotted by his brothers' gore;
Christians have Christians slain at his command,
 And, stainless priest and angel-like no more,
Joy might there be in Hell to see him stand
Thrust from the Altar-steps, an alien in the land.

v

Yet more condemned is he in his own soul.
 That ravished Psalter and his murdered friend,[1]
When cloud-like still these thoughts about him roll,
 May blot not out his sin, nor serve to fend
 His spirit from that fear which most can rend
A heart that loves—the Master's silent Face!
 Forgiven, restored, still must he fear that end—
The Eyes that looked on Peter fall'n from grace,
Which in their still reproach could more than sound
  abase.

VI

The Eyes that looked on Peter in the hall,
 The deep sad Eyes of wordless agony,
The Eyes of Love that love can most appal,
 Looked on him once again [2] beside the sea,

[1] See *A Short Life*, p. xxviii.
[2] St. John xxi. 15.

All changed save in their love's intensity :
And the long silence of that week's despair
    Brake then—to set the thrice-bound prisoner free ;
' *Behold My sheep, My lambs, once more thy care :*
Thou lov'st, then live again, My life, My death to
        share.'

VII

So when the time was full, meted in Heaven,
    And GOD had put that passionate heart to test,
And, as by fire, had purged its fiery leaven,
    Columba saw and heard.   The warrior crest
    Dust-humbled, shame-fast brow, and beaten breast
Felt the life-chrism of an angel's hand ;
    ' *Rest thou, thy slain have the eternal rest,*[1] '
From Abban's lips came as from Holy Land,
And with absolving power brake the last spirit-band.

VIII

Free he arose, and yet the more was bound :
    ' CHRIST'S man ' the more : CHRIST'S bondsman
        deeplier sworn
For farthest serving.   To th' absolving sound—
    In those sad ears the music of the morn—

---

[1] See *Short Life* p. xxix.

Sprang the old longing cry of one new born,
' *O Lord, my God,*[1] *what wilt Thou have me do ?* '
A cry self-answered in his soul's self-scorn :
' *Make dead thy life if thou would'st life renew ;*
Exile and slave art thou, if thou be freeman true.'

IX

Life : it was Erin ! field and flower and tree :
    Erin the beautiful, the emerald
Set on the right hand of the sovran sea :
    Erin the oak-groved and the mountain-walled :
    Mother august whose love her sons enthralled
As Zion hers ! where, earthly or divine,
    Sweet voices ever to sweet voices called :—
Life : it was Erin ! clan and throne and shrine ;
Of whom all thought and prayer ran in his veins like
    wine.

X

' *Not here my penance !* '   Met that inner cry
    The Hermit's[2] words, ' Men call thee here their
    own,
Here all things meet thine hand and court thine eye,
    And thou, beneath the shadow of a throne,

[1] Acts ix. 6.
[2] S. Molaisi (see *Short Life*, p. xxix.).

Ever art safe and never art alone ;
Not here the harvest-field of souls for thee :
Thou may'st not gather where thou hast not sown ;
Far from this love-encircled shore and sea,
For life repentance meet thy way and work must be.'

XI

He faltered not before the word of doom ;
  Nor turned his gaze from the far-pointing Hand
Of One Who stood before the gates of gloom ;
  And though the gesture was of stern command,
' *Follow thou Me*,' yet, as when first they scanned
Him He had named 'The Rock,' His regal eyes
  Were brimmed with love, so now the alien land
Became at once an altar and a prize :
Blest was that call in sooth that bade him agonise.

XII

Hard by an ocean towered a rock enthroned
  Crested with plumes that wantoned in the breeze,
And clad with flowers, the fairest summer owned ;
  Then fell the ruining plunge of sudden seas,
  And all that floral robe and crown of trees

Passed into wreck ; yet, statelier for the shock,
    In some new Spring, 'mid hum of homing bees
And bloom-bells ringing perfume, stood the rock,
While on its sunnier slopes fed a more beauteous
      flock.

XIII

So stood Columba's will—reft of its pride,
    Nobler for loss : renewed and consecrate :
Its outer self untameable had died,
    To be new-born in pangs, a worthier mate
    For form so fair.   Th' expanse of love and hate
Re-lived, not less: but 'twas a healthier sod,
    To be—by ruin's self regenerate—
Beneath the sunshine and the rains of God
For holier use and praise by men and angels trod.

XIV

Mark how Adamnan drew him in the light,
    Fronting the clear meridian of his quest,—
His limner leal as cunning—kingly height
    Of head and brows that towered o'er warrior
      breast,
    Crowned with such locks as sunshine loves for
      crest.

Yet more than monarch's was the angel mien
    Which spake a spirit by that SPIRIT blest
Who works by 'peace and love'—the Power unseen—
Neath passion's stormiest flood an ocean depth
    serene.

XV

Like ocean's too his voice [1]—deep as its roll
    Through Staffa's organ caves when winds are free,
A diapason wont to thrill the soul
    As charm the ear—yet soft as evening's sea
When winds are bound or wandering dreamily
Adown the funeral highway of the sun ;
    Voice like a poet's personality,
The power that wins the heart and holds it won,
That absent keeps its spell nor fails of work begun.

XVI

A Poet [2] he, by right divine of birth
    I' th' order rare, the dynasty of song—

---

[1] 'When singing in church with the brethren he raised his voice so wonderfully that it was sometimes heard four furlongs off: — yet to those who were with him in the church, his voice did not seem louder than that of others—it sounded the same far or near. . . . When, near the fortress of King Brudius, he chanted the evening hymns, some Druids did all they could to prevent . . . then he began to sing the 44th Psalm so wonderfully loud like pealing thunder . . . that king and people were struck with terror and amazement.'—Adamnan's *Life*, Book I. ch. xxix.

[2] The allusion here is not only to his merits as a poet—illustrated in a

A seer elect of mystic heaven and earth
  To whom the secrets of each shrine belong :—
  Yet with no poet-curse of bale or wrong :—
A joyous prophet with the regal smile
  And heartening glance, and sympathetic tongue
That, with all potent witchery but no guile,
Sad men with sorrow's self could sweetly reconcile.

XVII

The mood of noble natures, pessimist,
  Blinded to hope by the world-glare of ill :
Deaf to resultant good because they list
  The harsh remorseless grinding of that mill
  Whose grist is human lives set to fulfil
One fate of anguish or of failure ;—This,
  With all its inward agony, or the chill
Of sad or stoical silence, was not his :
He saw the Things to be now in the world that is.

XVIII

The mood of nobler natures, optimist,
  Whose will, the whole mazed world's uncounted
    woes

measure by the translations in this volume in the Appendix from pages 114
to 181—but to the fact that his powers of attraction were so great that he
may be called a 'king of men' by his wonderful winningness of manner and
the masterful influence of his personality.

And inexpressive shames—antagonist
   To hope not less than joy—cannot enclose
   From the high warrior purpose to oppose,
And the Saint's trust to win, was his : all wrong,
   And all the hordes of blatant fears and foes
Drowned not to him creation's undersong,
Prelude of final good, in hearts serene and strong.

XIX

Within no sternly narrowed course comprised,
   In stream of such clear mood ran Columb's
      thought
To issues broad and deep.   A world despised,
   Or rated by despair, shuns to be taught.
   The clay beneath the craftsman is not wrought
Frost-hardened : but if *he* be sun and rain,
   Forceful and tender, and his end be sought
With courage fed of faith, he shall attain
And mould to beauty's self his long-enduring pain.

XX

No marvel that men said the way he trod
   Calm as commanding, masterful as kind,
Was the old path of one who walked with God
   And with God's angels.   Crystal clear the mind :

Not for its tenderness of vision blind
To fault or failure : not by love enticed
From justice, though to love still most inclined,
And for his joy men knew one Fount sufficed :
A life thus cheerly lived was hid from self in
    CHRIST.

XXI

Careless of comfort : toiling hour by hour,
   Or with a ruler's brain, or artist's hand :
This in some miracle of penman's power,[1]
   The later scribe's despair—*that* in command
   Working his prophet-will o'er many a land,
As in his ' Family of Hy ' :[2] now lone
   In cell, or inland nook, or by sea-strand
   Wrestling in prayer :—or now, the angel flown,
Like the great Patriarch still, his rest one hallowed
   stone.[3]

[1] One of the duties of the monks of Iona and Lindisfarne was the copy-ing and illuminating of books. 'The book of Kells now in Dublin, and the Gospels of Lindisfarne now in the British Museum, still exist as bewildering witnesses to their skill with the pen. Nothing else comparable with these MSS. is known. How some parts of them were done without a microscope passes modern understanding.'—(Mr. WILLIAM MUIR'S *Life of St. Columba*, page 30.)

   In this art the Abbot himself was a master.

[2] Family of Iona : the community of the Island.

[3] The reputed stone pillow of St. Columba may still be seen in the Cathedral of Iona.

XXII

Thus souls innumerous rose to call him blest,
　　And those who wrought with him as feudal
　　lord.
Time fails to tell the reckoning of their quest—
　　To count the captives of each knightly sword
　　Brought to the feet of Him their soul adored.
Dark Albyn,[1] Isle and Highland, Scotia, Gaul,
　　Northland, Saxonia—on.　With one accord
They heard and flowed together at the call,
As he and his[2] for CHRIST did realm on realm
　　enthrall.

[1] See Note 3 in Preface, page xxiii.

[2] 'Such was the energy of the Celtic Missionaries that between the fifth and eighth centuries they had entered Gaul, Italy, Switzerland, and Germany; and even reached the Faroe Isles and Iceland; so that the Celtic Church extended from Iceland to Spain, from the Atlantic to the Danube, from Ireland to Italy.'—(BISHOP DOANE, U.S.A.)

Song: Columba and the Western Sea

I

Thou and thy sea are one
For ban or benison,
   Lords of your hour.
Slow will, sure end of tide :
   Law one with power,
Yet in its passion free—
A throned immensity
   Of calm or pride :—
Thou and thy sea are one.

II

Thou and thy sea are one :
Peers have ye princes none
   Of spirit change !
Can poet's eye and ear
   Find lordlier range,
Marking each mien and mood
   Of your infinitude,
   For love and fear ?
Thou and thy sea are one.

CANTO THE FIFTH

𝔗𝔥𝔢 ℜ𝔢𝔦𝔩𝔦𝔤 𝔒𝔯𝔞𝔫

I

Winds from St. Ronan's Bay[1] the Street of Death,
  Where in each Reilig[2] ridge rest by the Sound
Kings, Priests, and Chieftains. Each, of old, beneath
  The shade of its own Chantry wall, was crowned
  With its own Cross.   How, still, the sacred ground
Breathes Peace which, in the visionary mind,
  Blends with the ocean's and the sky's Profound!
And o'er these calm graves and mute hills behind
Hovers on dove-like wings soft on the sleeping wind!

---

[1] The bay beneath the village of Iona.

[2] The Reilig Oran (or Odhrain), which, as a place of sepulture, has been called the Westminster Abbey ground of Scotland, is described by the Dean of the Isles (1688), and from him by Buchanan, as originally consisting of three long ridges, each with its own chantry. One was inscribed: '*Tumulus Regum Scotiæ*,' where lie 48 Scottish monarchs beginning with Fergus II. and ending with Macbeth. (Cp. Shakespeare: *Macbeth*, Act II. Scene iv.:

    'Rosse.—*Where is Duncan's body?*
    Macduff.—*Carried to Colmskill,*
        The sacred storehouse of his predecessors
        And guardian of their bones.')

Another: '*Tumulus Regum Hiberniæ*,' where lie four Irish kings. And the third: '*Tumulus Regum Norwegiæ*,' containing eight kings of 'Norroway.'

II

Wait here a while.   Here, sooth, life's riddle seems
　　Less hard to solve.   A stern reality
Shows clear, albeit this is a land of dreams ;
　　Strong Purpose and meek Patience here agree
　　And Awfulness and Peace.   The sapphire sea,
The changeful heav'n, the wind-swept rocks, the tide,
　　In calm or passionate monotony,
Are with all memory of these hearts allied,
And what GOD so hath joined let no vain thought
　　divide.

III

Vain here to moan or moralise on death,
　　Where tombs of kings and priests tell of a life
Of force or use ; and the strong ocean's breath
　　Upon the brow or to the ear is rife
　　With bracing memories of splendid strife,
Or of adoring praise and ceaseless prayer.
　　Here Power the husband mates with Peace the
　　　wife,
And all high commune, and all earthly care
Make music mingling well on the twice-haunted air.

IV

Vain here the cynic's flout at place and power,
  The pomp of wealth, the pride of ancestry,
The brief distinctions of an earthly hour,
  The common fate of each inane degree,
  One end for all in one oblivion's sea;
The silence like a sealèd tomb of scorn;
  Without it nature's careless revelry;
Or round it cries of new contentions borne:
Once more the same fool's course, once more this
    close forlorn;—

V

For these were kings,[1] and sure the KING of kings
  Hath in His canon given their state His claim:

---

[1] The noble lines of Tennyson in the *Morte d'Arthur* are so apposite
that they might well have been written on this spot :—

> '*From the ruined shrine he stept
> And in the moon athwart the place of tombs,
> Where lay the mighty bones of ancient men,
> Old knights, and over them the sea-wind sang
> Shrill, chill, with flakes of foam.*'

And the preceding lines—

> '*He bore him to a chapel nigh the field,
> A broken chancel with a broken cross,
> That stood on a dark strait of barren land.
> On one side lay the ocean, and on one
> Lay a great water, and the moon was full,*'

are closely descriptive of the scene, if by ' the great water' the *Sound* is for
the moment understood instead of the *Lake*.

'Twas great to be at least *His* underlings,
　To bear the pale reflection of *His* name,
　Borne by them to more honour or more shame
As wielded each one well or ill his Rod—
　If passionate hearts were round them once aflame,
Who, as a cynic, treads this burial sod,
More base is he as man, more infidel to GOD.

VI

Baser as man : if whilom here the heart
　Of myriads pulsed with sea-like love or hate,
As each strong king or chief had borne his part
　For weal or woe—their blest or blighting fate,—
　If here such passions were articulate
To earth and heaven—a traitor, sure, is he,
　To all that makes our grovelling nature great,
With eyes too gross to mark, ascending free,
Incense of souls that burned on shrined humanity.

VII

Faithless to GOD yet more : no stolèd priest,
　Or mitred Bishop, here has fall'n on sleep,
But still his chant lives of the mystic East—
　Of GOD's descent upon the formless deep,

The void of souls—of Day-spring's upward leap—
Of Bethlehem, Calvary and Olivet,
  And that high Chamber where the downward sweep
Of that great Wind did for the CHRIST beget
That stately most sweet Bride who waits His coming
    yet.

VIII

Twice 'awful ground ';[1] if awe makes consecrate
  This Isle of the Evangel to the West,
Beyond all Isles, yet more importunate
  Is she, for reverence, here above this Rest,
  'Till the Day dawn,' of those her holiest,
Who wrought and prayed, and toiling still adored :
  Who stinted not of all their first and best
To make, as angels use, in heart accord,
By work to worship wed, meet offering to their LORD.

IX

Come thou not here, weak heart !   Muse, Poet, here :
  Here listen with thy soul.   Almost the roar
Of wind and wave is hushed upon thine ear,
  Now tuned to the low throbbing on the shore ;

---

[1] The expression of Dr. Johnson *in loco*.

Faint, first, and far listen a chanting soar
"Twixt Martyr's Bay and where the Holy Sign [1]
   Crowns the drear Road.   It swells the Sad Street
     o'er,
The bleak rocks and green hills and western brine,
As sorrow linked with death moves singing to the
     shrine.

x

Dull on the causeway sounds that measured tread
   Of warriors armed for pageant, not for fight :—
Sad pageant, closing a long glory, led
   By one prone form, pale as a norland night ;
   Yet see, within the shrine, the Altar's light
Touches with chrismal hope the sunken head,
   Until, re-issuing, after holiest Rite,
And the church-mother's latest Blessing said,
The old king sleeps at last sound in his Island bed ;

XI

Sleeps with his peers, the stateliest of their time,
   Of Albyn, Scotia, Norroway the far.
How dear soe'er, to each, ancestral clime,
   And claims of kin and clan, and scenes of war,

---

[1] That now known as Maclean's Cross.

Each old familiar vale or beetling scaur,
No Sleeping-place save this could serve him well ;
  Iona was his long life's pilot star,
Winning him home from native flood and fell
To make by Columb's side his safe monastic cell.

XII

Or, Poet, it may be thy musing hour
  May chance when all the firmament of air,
And sky and wave, are maddened by the power
  Of the weird Prince of fury and despair,
  And every violent spirit from its lair
Springs at his will, and screams across the sound
  With eyes of levin-flash, and flame-like hair,
And the torn seas like blasts of hail rebound
From each grey chantry wall and each sepulchral
    mound.

XIII

Well to thy musing fits this hour [1] of strife,
  If fancy to thy memory recall

---

[1] The allusion is to the conditions of weather at and after the death of
St. Columba.   Adamnan relates (Book III. ch. xxiv.) that he had predicted
that not a mixed multitude, but only his monks, should ' perform his funeral
rites and grace the last offices bestowed upon him.'
  Accordingly, immediately upon his death ' arose a storm of wind without

The seal of death set on a greater life,
   A more august and kinglier funeral :
   When the great Abbot lay beneath the pall ;
And all the seventy hours their lauds uprose—
   Well might his monks at every rise and fall
Deem that the spirits of the lost, in throes
Of anguish and despair, their cries did interpose.

XIV

Didst mark the instant [1] peace when all was done ?
   The strong winds bound, the deep sea still, the sky
A very smile of God, His benison
   On His elect ?   *They* seem to fail and die,
   And the loud world raves round them angrily ;
But heaven was open unto Stephen's gaze !
   For all the gnashing of their teeth, his eye
Was upon Jesus and those glory-rays :—
Then followed sleep and peace and soft amens of
    praise.

XV

' *The saints bore Stephen to his burial :*

   Then rose great persecution,' thus we read :

rain, which blew so violently during those three days and nights of his
obsequies that it entirely prevented any one from crossing the Sound. . . .'
   [1] 'And immediately after the interment of the Saint the wind ceased and
the whole sea became calm.'

Then read[1] we on how followed festival
  Of bliss and peace: the doomed of Satan freed,
  Sweet news of hope to souls in bitter need,
And joy in Heaven for such a gracious rain
  As woke on the waste lands the sleeping seed
For Harvest-Home. So wrought the Dead amain :—
So died Iona's chief, so lived his deeds again.

XVI

Where lies he now?   It is enough to know
  Though—as seven cities for their Poet's[2] birth—
Three kingdoms for this Prophet's bones may show
  High claim: though Albyn's,[3] Erin's, England's
    earth
For his last sleep would fain so shrine his worth,
Iona[4] *keeps his dust.*   There Columb lies
  Near all those Great within her Reilig's girth.
Thence when Eternal Spring makes open skies
Columb and Columb's men together shall arise !

---

[1] Acts viii. 1, 2, and 4, 5 to end.

[2] Homer.

[3] Saul, or Down, in Ireland, Dunkeld in Scotland, and Durham in England (see REEVES' *Life of St. Columba*, lxxxi. to lxxxiv.).

[4] 'The Grave of St. Columba is in Hy, where his remains were suffered to lie till a century had passed. Meanwhile his dust had mingled with the earth: and dust with dust continues there to this day.'—(REEVES, *ibid.*)

The Church Planets: A Hymn of the Union

OF THE ANCIENT CHURCHES OF GREAT BRITAIN AND THE CHURCHES COLONIAL AND AMERICAN

The historic line of light here indicated is that which—following the scattered lights that came from the East and the West to ancient Britain—came from Scotland to Ireland by St. Patrick, from Ireland to Scotland by St. Columba, thence to Northumbria by St. Aidan, and thence, by his successors, throughout the Heptarchy of England, and was united with the light from Italy and Gaul by St. Augustine, and is now extended, in Catholic unity, over the Asian, African, American, and Australasian world.

I

As to some lordly mountain
  Which o'er a broad land reigns,
Or some full river's fountain
  Which feeds the far-off plains,
When—praising GOD the Giver—
  Thy children's lauds arise,
Northumbria ! mount and river,
  To thee they lift their eyes.

II

Nigh lost,[1] Iona won thee—
  Isle of Saint Columb's cell—
Thence like new dawn upon thee
  His prophet[2] Blessing fell:
Thence came his saintly Aidan,
  As with the full day's smile,
With Western treasure laden
  Eastward to Holy Isle.[3]

III

Kings made thy good their glory:
  They gave thee of their best;
All time shall tell the story
  Of Oswald and his quest;[4]

[1] After the death of Edwin and the flight of Paulinus. On the other hand, it is fair to note in this connection the opinion of Canon Bright (*Early Church History*, ch. v. page 160). Commenting on Bishop Lightfoot's assertion that 'Aidan, not Augustine, was the Apostle of England,' he says: 'Aidan's relation to English Christianity as a whole has been somewhat seriously overrated . . . he cannot with anything like historical exactness be called the "Apostle of England."' See also note on p. 82.

[2] Columba's dying prediction from the Torr Abb of Iona.

[3] Lindisfarne, off the Northumbrian coast.

[4] King Oswald sent to Iona for a Bishop to revive Christianity in Northumbria, where only James, the Deacon of Akeburg, remained. Aidan was finally sent.

Of Hilda, in CHRIST's honour
 Won from her royal place,
Yet crowned with power upon her
 Of more than royal grace.

IV

How sing of each light-bearer
 Along the radiant line?
Each of one Sun the sharer,
 All from one centre shine;
With Austin's constellation,
 And old Saint David's flame;[1]
They showed the One Salvation,
 So name them by one name!

V

O SUN of Truth and Glory,
 With these who shone by Thee,
Shine other spheres[2] before Thee
 Past many a severing sea:
Each in his own course blessing
 Some far long-hidden land,

---

[1] The light of the ancient British Church in Wales was never quenched.
[2] Asian, African, Australasian, American. See Note 3, p. 10.

One CHRIST, one Creed confessing,
   Star-brethren of one band.

VI

Praise to our GOD for ever !
   Who these did call and send
Each to his own endeavour
   For one immortal end—
One Spiritual Nation
   'Neath one Eternal SUN,
The Church of our Salvation
   One in the THREE IN ONE.   Amen.

CANTO THE SIXTH

Aidan, Lindisfarne, and the Northumbrian Church

I

Ah, Blessed Dead, from labour resting well,
 How followed thee [1] thy works a thousand years,
And follow still, let old Northumbria tell
 And many a farther [2] region ! Cares and fears
 Sat not beside thy Celtic charioteers !
Meek Aidan, royal Oswald, how they rode
 Love-armoured through the phalanxes of spears
That stayed the fearful ; how their onset trode
Northumbria's darkness down in its elect abode !

[1] 'The Scotic Church may fairly claim that its work in the conversion of almost the whole of England was primary, not secondary ; was direct, not indirect ; came of its own impulse ; was not created by the stimulus of any of the three foreign missionaries, Augustine, Felix, Birinus.'—(BISHOP OF STEPNEY, *Conversion of the Heptarchy*, pp. 178, 179, 181.)

[2] In relation to the fact that a large part of the Continent was Christianised by Celtic Missionaries, Bishop Lightfoot says :—

'On the influence also of St. Columban, a Celtic contemporary of St. Columba (543-615), and his Celtic followers upon the evangelisation of Europe, see Montalembert's *Monks of the West*, ii. p. 387 *sq.*, Neander's *Church History*, v. p. 39 *sq.* He preached in France, Switzerland, and

II

' Blindness, heart-hardness, ignorance, drear array
    Of callous heathendom,' a doubter[1] cried,
' They yield not !' yet how soon the foemen lay
    In happy thrall to CHRIST ! Their king, their guide
    To his own King ; meek Aidan at his side :
True sons of thunder with those eyes of peace
    And tones of love that only conquer pride ;
Within whose only presence rancours cease,
And blind, imprisoned souls find vision and release.

III

So they proclaimed the ' Acceptable Year ' !
    While ' vengeance ' fell alone on chosen sin,
Bright spirits chased to hell the ghosts of fear,
    ' Beauty for ashes ' clothed the soul within ;
    And, as on angel wings, love entered in

Italy.   His principal monasteries were Luxeuil in the Vosges, and Bobbio near Milan.   St. Gall, on Lake Constance, was founded and named after his companion Gallus.   St. Columban first gave the impulse to the missionary enterprise in England and Ireland, which produced Cilian, Wilfrid, Willibrord, Willibald, Winfrid (Boniface), and many others.'—(*Leaders in the Northern Church*, p. 177.)

1 The first Missionary brought back to Iona a report of this sort.   It was Aidan who suggested in the conclave that by beginning with the use of ' the milk of more gentle doctrine, strength might follow for the reception and practice of God's more perfected and exalted counsel.'

Where misery and mourning ruled before ;
  Our larger England saw that Reign begin
Which the long years see widening evermore
O'er the immense new worlds and the far Austral
    shore.

IV

Greet we Iona's daughter, Lindisfarne,[1]
  The Holy Isle of the far Eastern sea,
Lone as a linden by a mountain tarn,
  Where rocks are drear and the storm winds blow
    free :
Yet—as the sunshine seeks the silver tree—

---

[1] ' From the cloisters of Lindisfarne,' writes Montalembert, 'and from the heart of those districts in which the popularity of ascetic pontiffs such as Aidan, and martyr kings such as Oswald and Oswyn, took day by day a deeper root, Northumbrian Christianity spread over the southern kingdoms. . . . What is distinctly visible is the influence of Celtic priests and missionaries everywhere replacing and seconding Roman missionaries, and reaching districts which their predecessors had never been able to enter. The stream of the Divine Word thus extended itself from north to south, and its slow but certain course reached in succession all the people of the Heptarchy.' And again, at the close of the chapters of which these are the opening words, he writes : ' Of the eight kingdoms of the Anglo-Saxon Confederation, that of Kent alone was exclusively won and retained by the Roman monks, whose first attempts among the East Saxons and Northumbrians ended in failure. In Wessex and in East Anglia the Saxons of the West and the Angles of the East were converted by the combined action of continental missionaries and Celtic monks. As to the two Northumbrian kingdoms, and those of Essex and Mercia, which comprehended in themselves more than two-thirds of the territory occupied by the German conquerors, these four countries owed their final conversion exclusively to the peaceful invasion of the Celtic monks.'

To her the grace of GOD drew softly down,
  Glad angels came and went unwearyingly,
And wove for it a spiritual crown
Which, next Iona's own, shines foremost in renown.

V

Isle of Saint Aidan,[1] where new toil begun—
  Which with his abbot's spanned the East and
    West—
And where[2] hard by, when the great work was done,
  His tired head, laid as on a mother's breast,
  Fell on sweet sleep—a happy warrior's rest—
If 'neath Iona's *thou* thy fame wouldst hide,
  As one but of another's right possessed,
Yet thou dost share her glory!   Celtic pride
Ranks sainted son with sire, like-statured, side by
    side.

---

[1] 'There, too, is Aidan' (says Bishop Lightfoot), 'the gentlest, simplest, most sympathetic, most loving, most devoted of missionaries—the rock whence we (Northumbrians) were hewn—the evangelist to whom before all others the English-speaking peoples owe not this or that benefit, but owe their very selves.'

[2] Twelve days after the news of King Oswyn's death was brought to him, he breathed out his soul, leaning against a buttress of the Church of Bamborough, a few miles south of Lindisfarne, August 31, 651. In the Calendar they called the day 'Quies Aidani,' Aidan's Rest : a 'tranquil close to a tranquil life : tranquil within, but most laborious without.'

VI

Yea, if to choose of sire or son the man
   The likeliest[1] framed to serve his fellows' weal,
Formed for his GOD upon the noblest plan,
   Were duty—there are those would set their seal
On son, not sire : not for more glowing zeal,
   A princelier purpose, or a heart more true :
But for calm spirit that could deeplier feel,
Eyes clearer to discern each tone and hue,
A patience finelier wrought to suffer and to do.

VII

A race new fall'n from faith how hard to move !
   As for the potter from dry clay to mould
Some vessel to the likeness of his love ;
   Seemed there the stream of heart-blood all too cold

---

[1] 'Measuring him side by side with other great missionaries of those days—Augustine of Canterbury, or Wilfred of York, or Cuthbert of his own Lindisfarne—we are struck with the singular sweetness, and breadth, and sympathy of his character. He had all the virtues of his Celtic race without any of its faults. A comparison with his own spiritual forefather—the eager, headstrong, irascible, affectionate, penitent, patriotic, self-devoted Columba, the most romantic and attractive of all mediæval saints—will justify this sentiment. He was tender, sympathetic, adventurous, self-sacrificing ; but he was patient, steadfast, calm, appreciative, discreet before all things. "This grace of discretion," writes Bede, "marked him out for the Northumbrian mission ; but when the time came he was found to be adorned with every other excellence." This ancient historian never tires of his theme when he is praising Aidan. "He was a man," he writes, "of surpassing gentleness and piety and self-restraint."'—(BISHOP LIGHTFOOT.)

For fresh warm life, its rocky channel old
Now sought at will once more, albeit the new
   Led to the fields of light and sands of gold ;—
Yet his this miracle ![1]   Apostle true,
Northumbria knows the fount where her heart-praise
    is due.

VIII

Iona sent, and Lindisfarne received,
   And on forlorn Bernicia spent the grace
Whereby for CHRIST the lost realm was retrieved,
   Fall'n, with her Edwin slain, from its high place
   When sad Paulinus passed and left no trace,
Save his great Deacon's[2] warrior work alone.
   Thee, nor thy Cross, Time's ravages efface,

---

[1] 'Not even the misconceptions of a controversial spirit can really question the fact that the Christian Church in Northumbria was built up by the steady painstaking work of the Scotic Church. James, the Deacon of Akeburg, had quietly stuck to his work near Catterick—but he was one man. . . . The feet of them that published the Gospel of Peace at large were Scotic feet. . . . The great bulk of England was brought to the Christian faith mainly through the influence of those who had learned all they knew from the Scotic Church.'—(BISHOP OF STEPNEY, *Conversion of the Heptarchy*, page 38.)

[2] In a chapter of great interest at the close of his *Conversion of the Heptarchy*, the Bishop of Stepney goes far to prove that the shaft of a cross in the churchyard of Hawkswell, five miles from Catterick, is an Anglo-Saxon one to the memory of Holy James, and that Akeburg was originally Jacob-burg, and that Hawkswell is from Yak's well, that is, Jacob's well: James's well.—(Pp. 215-219.)

F

Immortal James! and now, by Akeburg's stone,
Thee, the one faithful found, with loving praise we
  own.

IX

But save for thee,[1] remained nor Holy Sign,
 Nor Church, nor Altar, betwixt Forth and Tees:
So where heart-sickened Rome had ceased to shine
 Shone Scotia from Iona. 'Hoarse the seas,'

---

[1] The story of Paulinus, in relation to Northumbria, begins as beautifully as it ends sadly. It is, shortly, this:—He was one of the four monks sent by Gregory from Rome in 601 in aid of Augustine. At the court of Edwin he was chaplain to his Christian wife Ethelburga. An escape of the king and the birth of a daughter influenced the king, under Paulinus, towards Christianity, and after the Witan in the next winter—when the remarkable scenes occurred, first, of the comparison, by one of his warriors, of human life to the flight of a sparrow into and out of a banquet hall at winter-tide; and next, of Coifi, the heathen priest, taking the lead in the desecration of the heathen temple—the king and his nobles were baptized, and, subsequently, multitudes of the people. But the work must have been superficial or ill-organised. The present Bishop of London, Dr. Creighton, thus comments on it in a Lecture this year (1897) at Salisbury: 'The people were baptized in masses, the consequence being that when another king arose (after the slaying of Edwin) Christianity entirely disappeared, and Paulinus had to run away, ending his days as Bishop of Rochester.' Then, to quote from the words of the Bishop of Stepney (*Church Bells*, June 3, 1897): 'Oswald and his brothers of the Bernician branch of the royal family of Northumbria, who had been converted by the Scotic Church of Iona, drove out the Britons who had conquered Edwin, and made the land English and Christian again; and by their friendships and alliance with other sovereigns they introduced Christianity to almost the whole of the remaining parts of "England" other than Kent and East Anglia, and the whole of their Christianising work was done by those who brought them to Christ, the Scotic school of Columba.' Bede says: '*Nullum fidei Christianæ signum, nulla ecclesia, nullum altare erectum est, priusquam hoc sacræ crucis vexillum novus militiæ ductor contra hostem immanissimum*

The poet[1] sings, that gird the ' Hebrides,'
But sweet the sound that from the barren Isle
   Bore the great Name along the Northern leas,
And soft the light on England, dimmed a while,
That shone with love reborn in Aidan's saintly smile.

X

A song and smile that grew and never died :
   Oh, beautiful upon our English hills
The feet of those isle heralds !   They abide
   Yet on our paths of peace.   Our England thrills
   Yet with the Celtic tread, and yet she fills
Her holy vessels at the wells of light,
   Themselves full filled of old from Eastern rills
That westward flowed through the primæval night
From Siloah's healing fount 'neath Salem's[2] mountain
   height.

---

pugnaturus statueret.—(*Hist. Eccl.* iii. 2.) On the other hand, Canon Bright (*Early Church History*, p. 149, 1897) writes : ' It has been too much the fashion to speak of the work of Paulinus as utterly ruined by the catastrophe of Hatfield. . . . The Northumbrian Christians were " cast down but not destroyed." '

[1] Longfellow.

[2] The source of Celtic Christianity was most probably not from Rome of the West, but from the Church of Jerusalem. (See note, p. 100.)

XI

Was ever galaxy of nobler names
　　Than stars the expanse of old Northumbrian skies?
No comet-mists or passing meteor flames,
　　Like burst of song that quickly soars and dies;
　　Slowly, serenely, steadfastly they rise:
Immortal music with their orbit swells:
　　Each calmly gazes as with angel eyes:
Each in his sphere his heavenly tidings tells;
Deep as true love their sound, and sweet as evening
　　　bells.

XII

His Twelve [1] with Aidan—sons of love and war,—
　　Lovers of souls, they led the wars of God;—
His Oswald, more than monarch evermore,
　　With whom the Heavenfield Cross [2] was kingly rod,

[1] One of S. Aidan's beginnings of work was the gathering about him and training a body of twelve young men, many of them afterwards famous. One of these was Eata, who followed him in the Bishopric of Lindisfarne; and the two brothers Cedd and Chad, and Wilfrid, 'the most famous of Northern Churchmen in a succeeding age.'

[2] 'Heavenfield, a spot not far from Hexham, was the place where Oswald's few met the vast host of Cadwalla—"the hero of a hundred fights"—and defeated them and slew Cadwalla. With his own hands before the battle he planted a Cross in the ground, holding it as the soldiers filled in the earth. Then he and his army went to prayer. It was "*Hoc signo vinces*" over again, but in the case of a nobler Christian and a manlier king.

Who sang his Alleluia till he trod
The warrior's highway to a throne more blest,
   Leaving his martyr seed upon the sod ;
Then Oswyn, with the Cross too on his breast,
Whose sleep on stricken field won his true Aidan [1]
    ' rest.'

XIII

And thou, imperial Hilda,[2] dove-like soul,
   Yet eagle-winged : men's counsellor and guide,
Strength to the strong, as ivy round the bole,
   Or as the enchaining of the flood of tide
   Holds the long shore.—Caedmon is at thy side ;
O Morning Star [3] o' the morning stars of song,
   From thee our poet ages are allied
These more than thousand years—that choric throng
Whose music rolls in light our English heavens along !

---

[1] See Note 2 on p. 79.

[2] Hilda was a princess of the Northumbrian royal family. She became, under Aidan, one of the chief educators of the Northumbrian Church. Her monastic house became a great training-school for clergy, and she herself was often consulted by princes and bishops, and she was specially called ' Mother,' from her piety and grace. None more than she have been true ' Mothers' in Israel.

[3] It was Hilda who encouraged Caedmon the cowherd to become the earliest English poet. It is in connection with this fact that Bishop Lightfoot finely says (*Leaders in the Northern Church*, p. 67) : ' Here English literature was cradled. The earliest of English poets, Caedmon, the forerunner of Chaucer and of Shakespeare, of Spencer and of Milton, of Wordsworth and Tennyson and Browning, received under Hilda the training and the

XIV

Cedd, Chad and Cuthbert, Wilfrid, Biscop, Bede,
    Egbert and Albert, cultured Alcuin [1]—
For Church and country chieftains good at need,
    Northumbria's sons and saints, your memories win
    Deathless heart-praise !—But, as ye pass, begin
More than the ruin and fire that from the foam
    With the fierce Dane upon your shrines poured in :
So slowly, surely the free Island Home
Lies like a thing in trance, in charm of 'later Rome.'

XV

The body, not the spirit !   'Neath the spell
    Of outer bondage struggled the free soul : [2]
And many a sign and many a word would tell
    The chafing 'neath the never loved control ;

inspiration which transformed him, like Amos of old, from a simple cowherd into a prophet and teacher of men. If English poetry, in its power, its variety, its richness, surpasses the poetry of any other nation of the modern, perhaps even of the ancient world, if it be one of God's most magnificent literary gifts to mankind, then we must contemplate with something like reverential awe the house where it was nursed in its infancy.'

[1] For an admirable account of these workers, see a short work published by the S.P.C.K., *Northumbrian Saints*, by the Rev. E. C. S. Gibson. See also the great work of Canon Bright, *Chapters of Early Church History*, third edition, 1897.

[2] 'Through the long ages of Roman domination the English Church was the least enslaved of all the Churches. Her statute-book is a con-

Still could it faintly hear the ocean-roll !
Still dimly see the far-off cradle Isle :
Still mark the raised hands on the 'Abbot's Knoll';
At Columb's living voice or Aidan's smile,
Glamours of that new claim would lose their powers
    a while !

XVI

Slowly and surely as the spell begun,
    Slowly and surely passed its charm away ;
Then—sudden shock before the break of sun !
    Before—as rise the mists at matin ray—
    Each looked on each as in the old clear day ;
And though the lands with many a wreck were strewn,
    And many a frenzied soul went far astray,
Yet most, like men who wake at last from swoon,
Looked to that rock at last from which they had been
    hewn.

.   .   .   .   .

tinued protest against this foreign aggression. Her ablest kings were the resolute opponents of Roman usurpation. When the yoke was finally thrown off, though the strong will of the reigning sovereign was the active agent, yet it was the independent spirit of the clergy and people which rendered the change possible. Hence there was no break in the continuity of the English Church. Of this independent spirit, which culminated in the Reformation, Aidan, our spiritual forefather, as we have seen, was the earliest embodiment.'—(BISHOP LIGHTFOOT.)

XVII

Iona the recluse, not lordly Rome,
    Iona of the primal purity,
Was nursing mother,[1] England, in thine home :
      Was most about thee in thine infancy—
      Isle of the open sky and crystal sea ;—
If she of the stern hills and turbid wave
    Sent of her best and stateliest to thee
By Gregory, the loving and the brave,
Yet largelier e'en than they thine Island mother gave.

XVIII

Thou art not Rome's, my England. As I stand
    Fronting Iona's waters, and the wind
Blows free upon my face, and the rock-land
    Is firm beneath my feet, and all my mind
    Is joyous with the great things set behind
And the great hope before, well do I know
    In deep of heart that he were fool and blind
Who sees not whence thy faith and freedom flow,
And where by grace of God thy royal banners go.

---

[1] 'I will show you the cradle of your race. The time is the middle of the sixth century. The scene is a lonely island off the western coast, beaten by the Atlantic surge. This Iona—this bleak, barren patch of land—is the spiritual and intellectual metropolis of Western Christendom. Here is the centre of civilisation, of learning, of light and truth for the nations.'—(BISHOP LIGHTFOOT, p. 109.)

XIX

O great Church-Mother, forward, o'er the world
  Of farthest seas and continents, they go !
And, as to all the blasts they fling unfurled,
  Iona's legend ever bid them show,
  Bright in the matin gleam or vesper-glow,
Truth, Peace, and Love :—the old simplicity
  August in beauty the divinest !   Lo,
The wide earth beckons and th' 'inviolate sea' :
' Forward, Iona's child, Church-Mother of the free ! '

A Morning on Iona

A SONG

A tender mist of amber lawn,
Aurora's vesture ere the dawn,
A robe already half-withdrawn
    O'erhung the heaving bay;
Just might be seen beneath its pall
Her bosom's restful rise and fall:
Just heard from far the breezy call
    That summoned up the day.

The amber deepened into gold:
Then softly, slowly, fold by fold,
The lingering robe away she rolled:
    Then, smiling sleep to scorn,
To sound of wings the waste along
That woke the ripples into song,
A goddess, beautiful and strong,
    Up leapt the living Morn!

CANTO THE SEVENTH

On the Torr Abb

I

A Paraphrase of the Prophecy of St. Columba on the 'little Hill'
on the last evening of his life, June 8th, 597 A.D.

' *Albeit, Iona, thou art small and poor,*
   In all the mighty world so mean a thing,
The spirit that is of thee shall allure
   The love of many a people, many a king.
   Not Scotia only shall her homage bring,
But the barbarians of a world unknown
   Shall make to thee their reverent offering,
And Saints of Churches far away shall own
The small become so great, this mean Isle made a
   throne.'

.   .

II

Come, Poet, this still hour, past evensong,
   Noon's rainy passion charmed away.   A while

Stand here upon Torr Abb.   Before thee throng,
   Like archangelic warders of the isle,
   White, columned clouds, ascending, pile on pile,
From sea and mountain bases to such height
   As shuts the world away, yet wins the smile,
Behind Duni, of the last lingering light,
Day's norland benison to fade not through the night.

III

They stand, these misty spires, as, for the hour,
   Recalling by high symbol to the mind,
In their august array, the mystic power,
   Which in a circle of sure truth enshrined
   The vaunt wherewith the passing Saint divined—
(This Monticellulus the pulpit stone
   For this, his dying oracle, assigned)—
That the mean Isle should be a future throne
For homage paid by lands the far-off and unknown.

IV

This is Iona's heart.   Here as we muse
   The grey Cathedral ruins[1] melt away ;

---

[1] All the ruins in Iona are of buildings 500 years later than the Columban
time.

All relics of a thousand years we lose
   'Twixt this Torr Abb and ghostly Martyrs' Bay.
   Nought meets our eyes save of her earlier day—
Her Abbot's church, its own cross sentinel,
   The plain monastic huts in quaint array,
And as to worship calls the evening bell
We see the brethren pass each from his lowly cell.

V

The bell has ceased.   The hush is yet more still,
   A deep-voiced tremor on th' adoring air
Floats slowly to our ears upon the hill—
   Listening as if th' o'erwatching angels there
   With folded plumes themselves were bowed in
      prayer—
Until it swells and heightens into song,
   A laud exultant over sin and care,
Sonorous as an ocean-voice and strong,
Adown the shoreward lea, the island wastes along.

VI

We see not now yon Nunnery.[1]   Our heart,
   Behind it fifty decades, visions there,
As here, low cells and shrine of simpler art,
   And monks of thew and sinew as of prayer,

[1] See note on preceding page.

Who make the world's lost sheep as much their
    care
As their own souls : bondsmen, yet free, and fain
    In shepherding right soldierly to fare
O'er field and mount, o'er flood and frozen main ;
On such crusaders strong what captive calls in vain ?

VII

With laud and orison thus to wake the night
    And greet the morn, and keep each sacred hour,
Is rule that sweetens with unearthly light
    The hard long day, and makes each cell a bower
    Of spiritual vine and amaranth flower ;—
Yet are they built, too, on a warrior's plan,
    They stand their height, complete in all their
        power,
As if round each one's life this legend ran :
CHRIST'S thrall in noblest wise since every inch a man.

VIII

Mark thou the vigorous life of every day :
    No hanging hands are here, or feeble knees.
They know to reap the harvest of the bay,
    As of the plough—to climb the breaking seas,

Or stem the tide against the northern breeze;

Their fasts but curb the flesh, not bow the form;

Firm set are they as their own Hebrides:

Cool in the solstice, in the ice-blast warm:

At home in deep or height, strong children of the
    storm.

IX

A wholesome life 'twixt constant prayer and toil!

And when from far the fuller calling came,

And the monk-missioner for larger spoil

Followed the summons of some beacon flame,

Signalling ghostly need in the great name,

He passed as some tried athlete, or as knight

At all points armoured against fear or shame:

High couraged, strong of limb and keen of sight,

As he was pure of heart and dweller in the Light.

X

Ruled over each—as charity[1] clothes all—

The sweet stern spirit of a love so tender,

So simple-strong—since ever musical

To one high note of truth—that all the splendour,

[1] Coloss. iii. 14.

Which art or culture or proud claim can render
To their elect, with it can never vie
    As mover, or inspirer, or defender,—
And was to each his shining panoply,
Wherein he went his way to do and dare and die.

XI

Such were Saint Columb's sons on whom that eve
    From the Torr Abb he gazed, as work or prayer
Held them beneath him.   Could he but believe
    That the great heart that beat before him there
    Had for high quest a path whereon to fare
Beyond all thought or vision, only known
    By Him Who willed Iona should prepare
A way among the nations for His own,
Where He would plant His Cross and rear His
        Altar-Throne?

XII

What saw the Dying, as he prophesied
    Here with uplifted hands—one towards the East,
Whence flowed of light and grace the fontal tide—
    One Westward?   Haply, to the visioned Priest,
    O'er that enormous water-world there ceased

(Gave GOD such guerdon to his soul?) the spell
   Sundering so long earth's vastest from its least—
Those vastest shores from which the surges swell,
From this small speck on sea, this poor Saint
    Columb's cell.

XIII

Mark, pilgrim, four [1] who stand beside thee here,
   From those far lands beyond the desert seas,
With more than the bland tourist's eye and ear [2]
   Of vapid, or of vainly-acted, ease,
   The mask of ignorance or languor: these—
Owning a contrast of true voice and mien—
   With what crown'd hope and solemn sympathies
They look with fervour on the reverent scene,
Not less for what shall be than what has greatly been!

XIV

They bow as 'neath a Blessing.   Inward sight
   O'erflies yon mighty waters rolling Home,
And sees their brethren standing in the light
   'Neath the one Church's vast Cathedral dome:
They hear those voices overleap the foam,

---

[1] Visitors from America.
[2] See Wordsworth's sonnet, 'Cave of Staffa.'

Crying, ' We are Iona's—Columb's men !
    Ye stand beside our cradle, ye who roam ;
Keep us, O brothers, keep us in your ken,
Blest now beneath Torr Abb, as in our fathers then !'

XV

Poet, bow too beneath it :—Unto Faith
    These fifty generations are a day :
Those who believe not, see here but a wraith,
    Catch but faint echoes of a long lost lay :
    For them the Church grows like the old world
        grey :
But not to Faith.   The Word, the Creeds, the Line
    Were, and will be,—nor Time's nor Schism's prey,—
To Her ' the gifts and calling ' are Divine ;
Here still Saint Columb stands and blesses still his
        shrine.

XVI

Not less with Her lives Hope than Memory,
    What sundering tides between may seem to roll ;
Ever her forward gaze is rapt and free ;
    Ruin and wreck may grieve, not daunt her soul,
    Nor death ring there a never-ceasing toll ;

Far on in vision, let who will despair,
  Ever her chariot rounds a further goal ;
Brave prisoner in hold ! her ears are 'ware,
And catch, past dungeon-grate, free voices on the air.

XVII

She sees at Port-na-Churaich a new sail ;
  Again commissioned feet spring on the shore, [1]
The old liturgic antiphons prevail
  Over the sea-wind and th' Atlantic roar,
  And blend with either as they sink or soar ;
Again a Bishop at his Altar stands :
  Th' Eternal Offering is shown once more ;
Above the old grey rocks and silver sands
A cynosure reborn Iona fronts the lands.

XVIII

Come, Day, that will'st come ! Tarry not, but come !
  All holy sound and solemn scene attending !
Thine Albyn's children once again at home :
  To their first Pentecostal Altar wending :
  Old Gaelic praise from Gaelic heart ascending

1 See Sonnets, ' Bishop's House,' pp. 101, 102.

Tuned to the Celtic rite and Catholic Creed ;
  Child-West[1] once more i' th' ancient worship
    blending
With Mother-East which first her spirit freed :—
That first Faith hers once more, she shall be free
  indeed.

[1] 'At the Synod of Whitby the Celtic Church claimed to follow the practice of the East and of the Apostle St. John, from whom they said their forefathers had derived their customs. . . . This is a corroborative proof that the origin of their Church was Oriental. . . . We think that now the question of origin may be set at rest, and that the verdict is in favour of their Eastern descent.'—(BISHOP EWING, *Iona and the Early Celtic Church*, chap. xiii. pp. 38, 39.)

SONNETS

The 'Bishop's House' in Iona

TO ALEXANDER

LORD BISHOP OF ARGYLL AND THE ISLES

(From *The Guardian*, June 1896)

' The gifts and calling of God are without repentance.'—ROM. xi. 29.

I

Father in GOD, of that unchanging line
    Varying, mayhap, in station or in case,
    But not in rule or creed, or in that grace
Of hands that seal or send by right Divine :
Lo, here for visible authentic sign
    Of that which man may but a while displace,
    And ruining time can never all deface,
Thy House of peace and consecrated Shrine !
Once more an altar by Saint Columb's cell—
    The old ' Vexillum Regis ' on its tower—
    Once more the ordering hands that send with
        power,
And keys that ope and keep the citadel,
And voices to proclaim by changeless Creed,
' Without repentance ' are GOD's gifts indeed !

II

Witness, ye old unchanging seas and skies
   That vary, yet are evermore the same—
   Skies, now serene, now rent by levin flame,
Seas, like the sun, that ever fall and rise,
Yet in all case secure and in all guise :—
   And ye, eternal hills, whose antique claim
   Puts things that pass, vaunting their hour, to
      shame—
By all that doth your state immortalise,
Witness—Ye saw Columba's Pentecost,
   Ye heard his chanted *Gloria*, and his Creed,
   And Eucharist with his twelve. Oh, by this
      rede,
Witness, GOD's gifts and calling are not lost !
By these fair firstfruits point the promise plain
That CHRIST's One Church shall have her own
      again.

Farewell

OFF STAFFA : IONA IN THE DISTANCE :

A RAINY SUNSET, SEPT. 29, 1896

Poeta peregrinus loquitur

I

Yonder the Church's fane : here Nature's shrine :
   And Both of GOD.   Here in yon awful cave—
The more, because of no man's art, divine—
   Like some vast concourse through Cathedral nave,
   Past the weird columns to their architrave,
Rolls the Atlantic's multitudinous tread
   In Prime and Vesper worship, wave on wave :
Till Reverence here might kneel with lowliest head,
While Fancy feigned within some antique Altar
    dread.

II

Yonder Iona ;—If my heart a while
   On Staffa's waters, at this parting hour,
Greets fixedly this weird mysterious isle
   Whereon th' Unknown and Immemorial lower

Most in this world,—'tis but a while.—The power,
'That makes our God-indwelt humanity
　Time's Sovereign, wins me back to yonder tower,
To yonder shore slow sinking on our lee,
Iona's holier fane and more immortal sea.

III

Iona, dear Iona !　Lingeringly
　The Isle to sight dies with the sun.　Appears
Yet one faint glory far upon Duni,
　While all this Staffa sea is drowned in tears.
　Albeit ' Farewell ' be sealed by all the years
Of this fast-fading life, yet, O my soul !
　Sure art thou that on dying eyes and ears,
For all high hope, for true love's passing toll,
Iona's heavens shall smile, Iona's waters roll.

APPENDIX

English Prose Translation of the (reputed) Rule of Columcille[1]

The rule of Columcille beginneth.

1. Be alone in a separate place near a chief city, if thy conscience is not prepared to be in common with the crowd.

2. Let a fast place, with one door, enclose thee.

3. Be always naked in imitation of CHRIST and the Evangelists.

4. Whatsoever little or much thou possessest of anything, whether clothing, or food, or drink, let it be at the command of the senior, and at his disposal, for it is not befitting a religious to have any distinction of property with his own free brother.

[1] First printed by Dr. Reeves from an MS. in the Burgundian Library at Brussels, with a translation by the late Professor O'Curry, in the Appendix to Primate Colton's *Visitation of Derry*, printed for the Irish Archæological Society. It was again printed in *Hadden and Stubb's Councils*, vol. ii. p. 119, from which it is now copied.—(*Life of St. Columba,* by Rev. E. A. COOKE.)

The Same: in Poetical Paraphrase

1. Hard by where men in some chief city dwell,
   If loneness with thy soul accordeth well,
   Alone, for work or prayer, make thou thy cell.

2. Thy fastness it shall be, behind, before,
   Thy hold of prayer ; save for its single door
   It shall from men enclose thee evermore.

3. Naked shall be thy life of earthly pelf ;
   This shalt thou duly order for thyself
   To be as CHRIST and His Apostles Twelve.

4. Befits not thee that ought thou hast be thine,
   Save at thine Abbot's will.   Food, clothing,
       wine
   Must be thy brethren's too i' the life divine.

5. A few religious men to converse with thee of GOD and His Testament; to visit thee on days of solemnity; to strengthen thee in the Testaments of GOD and the narratives of the Scriptures.

6. A person too who would talk with thee in idle words, or of the world; or who murmurs at what he cannot remedy or prevent, but who would distress thee more, should he be a tattler between friends and foes, thou shalt not admit him to thee, but at once give him thy benediction should he deserve it.

7. Let thy servant be a discreet, religious, not tale-telling man, who is to attend continually on thee, with moderate labour of course, but always ready.

8. Yield submission to every rule that is of devotion.

9. A mind prepared for red martyrdom.
A mind fortified and steadfast for white martyr-dom.

10. Forgiveness from the heart to every one.
Constant prayers for those who trouble thee.

5. Few friends but fervent, of divine accord
   And power to commune with thee of the LORD,
   His Fasts and Feasts and Testamental Word.

6. Avoid a talker plaintive of his woes,
   An idle tattler between friends and foes—
   Yet if not worthless bless him ere he goes.

7. Devout shall be thy servant and discreet;
   No idle prattler: constant, faithful, fleet;
   No toilworn slave, yet for all service meet.

8. Let this obedience willing be, and whole;
   To constant sacrifice of heart and soul
   By the set hours thou shalt thyself control.

9. Let never fear in thy brave heart find home:
   Calm, let it front whatever crisis come,
   Be it the red or the white martyrdom.

10. In patience be content to suffer long;
    In all-forgiving charity be strong,
    Constant in prayer for all who do thee wrong.

11. Fervour in singing the office for the dead, as if every faithful dead was a particular friend of thine. Hymns for souls to be sung standing.

12. Let thy vigils be constant from eve to eve, under the direction of another person.

13. Three labours in the day, viz. prayers, work, and reading.

14. The work to be divided into three parts, viz. thine own work, and the work of thy place as regards its real wants; secondly, thy share of the brethren's work;

15. Lastly, to help thy neighbours, viz. by instruction, or writing, or sewing garments, or whatever labour they may be in want of, ut Dominus ait, 'Non apparebis ante me vacuus.'

16. Every thing in its proper order; Nemo enim coronabitur nisi qui legitime certaverit.

11. With form erect to God and earnest tongue,
    As if thou wert thine heart's elect among,
    Thine office for the dead in Christ be sung.

12. Thy vigils on from eve to eve shall be,
    And, as thy guardian, let another see
    That duly each in course be kept by thee.

13. Three toils for thee must consecrate the day :
    In triple duty portion all thy way :
    As thou must work, so must thou read, and pray.

14. In sections three thou shalt the work divide :
    For work of thine, and of thy place, provide :
    Next, be with thine thy brother's claim allied ;

15. Last, let thy neighbour's needs as thine be dear :
    Teach, write, or sew: the Master's word is clear:
    ' Empty before Me thou shalt not appear.'

16. By settled law and order seek thine end :
    'Tis writ, ' Him only will the Judge commend
    Who shall according to His rule contend.'

17. Following almsgiving before all things.

18. Take not of food till thou art hungry.
Sleep not till thou feelest desire.
Speak not except on business.

19. Every increase which comes to thee in lawful meals, or in wearing apparel, give it for pity to the brethren that want it, or to the poor in like manner.

20. The love of GOD with all thy heart and all thy strength.
The love of thy neighbour as thyself.
Abide in the Testaments of GOD throughout all time.

21. Thy measure of prayer shall be until thy tears come; or thy measure of work of labour till thy tears come; or thy measure of thy work of labour or of thy genuflexions until thy perspiration often comes, if thy tears are not free.

17. Within, without, as thou would'st perfect be,
　　Let men take knowledge that they find in thee
　　The heart and hand of holiest charity.

18. For thy due gain eat only, not for greed:
　　Sleep not except when thou hast very need:
　　Nor may'st thou speak except for cause indeed.

19. Thine increment of raiment or of food
　　Shall be at service of the brotherhood,
　　Or for the poorer alien's gain and good.

20. Love GOD to all thy being's depth and height:
　　With thine own weal thy neighbour's still unite:
　　Walk heavenward in the one Word's double light.

21. Even to tears give prayer and toil their space;
　　And, if tears fail thee, let thy sweat of face
　　Mark thy devotion's zeal and meed of grace.

St. Columba's Prediction

(Attributed)

GAELIC

An I mo chridhe, I mo graidh
An aite guth manaich bi'dh geum ba ;
Ach mun tig an suoghai gu crich
Bithidh I mar a bha.

ENGLISH PARAPHRASE

Iona of my heart and love !
　The kine shall low where swelled our strain ;
But ere the Lord come from above
　Thy Church shall have her own again !

Derry: A Song of St. Columba

BELOVED is Raphoe the pure:
   Beloved are Kells and Drumhome:
But sweeter and fairer to me
The salt breezes fresh from the sea,
   The cry of the gulls on the foam,
   When homeward to Derry I come—
To the oak-groves of Derry, from far,
Where GOD's angels in multitude are.

Fair Derry, for thee and for thine,
I would give—if all Erin were mine
From its centre right on to its strand—
I would give all the wealth of the land
   ' For thine and for thee,
O thou fairer and sweeter to me,
     Sweeter to me!

St. Columba's Song of Trust[1]

I

I TREAD the mountain passes through the gloom

Alone, save that Thy Presence can illume,

Sun of my soul! these rough ways of the night,

And turn the fearsome darkness into light.

II

Should that day dawn—the last that I should see—

No mightiest aid could save from Thy decree:

No valley fastness or embattled hill

Sure ward could keep against Thy sovereign will.

III

Man! if thou art *not* GOD's, e'en at His shrine,

Or in some vale of rest, death may be thine;

If thou *art* GOD's, thou can'st not be death's prey

E'en in the front and fury of the fray.

[1] A prose translation is given in *The Life of St. Columba*, by William Muir and the Rev. J. C. Kendell.

IV

What is our life?   It is our FATHER'S will,

Or brief or long, of seeming good or ill ;

Who risk may save, who guard may cast away ;

The proudest front not fate with ' yea ' or ' nay.'

V

Ah, living GOD ! who worketh ill or wrong

Treadeth a path that haunting terrors throng ;

The hopes his bosom fondles waste in air,

And o'er his future broods eterne despair.

VI

No magic mirror may mine end foretell,

No bird in bush sing fortune's oracle ;

In Thee alone, my Father, I will trust,

GOD, evermore the Faithful and the Just.

VII

O CHRIST, the SON, my Prophet, King Divine

Yet human, born of Mary—Master mine—

O FATHER and blest SPIRIT, One-in-Three,

All that I am and have I trust to Thee.   Amen.[1]

[1] The following is closer to the original :—
> O CHRIST, the SON, my Druid, King Divine
> Yet human, born of Mary, Abbot mine—
> O FATHER and blest SPIRIT, One-in-Three,
> My lands, my Order I entrust to Thee.   Amen.

'𝔘𝔠𝔥𝔡 𝔄𝔦𝔩𝔲𝔦𝔫': 𝔄 𝔖𝔬𝔫𝔤 𝔬𝔣 𝔖𝔱. ℭ𝔬𝔩𝔲𝔪𝔟𝔞 [1]

I

UCHD AILUIN, Uchd Ailuin !
  Oh, for thy rocks and thee :
Therefrom to gaze, thereon to hear
  The high song of the sea :
The wild waves' lay, that lauds for aye
  Our FATHER's majesty.

II

Sweet on the diamonded strand
  To see the sunlight blaze,
And, while the rolling breakers lift
  The thunder of their praise,
To rest and hear the bird-chant clear
  That fills the woodland ways.

---

[1] The original is in one of the Irish MSS. in the Burgundian Library at Brussels. It is quoted by the Rev. E. A. Cooke from *Celtic Scotland*.

III

There would I watch the shepherding
    O' the white flocks of the sea:
And wondrous monsters of the waves
    In frolic sporting free:
What time the roar blends on the shore
    With holier minstrelsie.

IV

But 'Cul-ri-Erin' must I hear
    Sound like a mystic name:
Hear it with the in-flowing tide,
    And with the ebb the same:
The healing smart of my sad heart,
    My honour and my shame.

V

The sins I mourn innumerous,
    Like wave on wave they roll—
Stern memory on memory—
    As they would whelm my soul:
Yet will I trust the Good, the Just,
    Who doth the worlds control.

VI

Now may I find on holy page
    All for my spirit's weal :
Now to the Heaven that holds my heart
    I would adoring kneel :
Now in high praise the sweet song raise
    That most may soothe and heal.

VII

Now would I meditate the things
    That touch my Chief, my King :
Now would the Orders in His Heavens
    Fill my imagining :
Now would I know how things below
    May each its solace bring.

VIII

Food in rock crannies would I find
    And harvest in the deep.
Blest is the freeman's toilsome day :
    And still more blest than sleep
In quiet cell ere Matin bell
    A holy watch to keep.

IX

The poor of Christ would still be mine,
  To find as me He found :—
Ah, kindness of my God and King !
  His Presence wraps me round
With Grace and Peace that yet increase
  And yet shall more abound.

From Erin to Albyn: A Song of St. Columba

I

To gallop with those peerless steeds,
    White coursers of the main,
When the wild water highway leads
    Erin, to thee, again :—
Such joy was mine !—to see them leap
    With glinting manes of foam
Along the strand or up the steep
    That ring my island home.

II

Now, sternward far fair Derry lies !—
    To yonder alien strand
Bow-ward I turn these sad grey eyes
    To thee, the Raven's land :—
Albyn, to thee ! with tears full fain
    Should they look back once more,
Yet never will they greet again
    The old belovèd shore.

III

The Albyn ravens bid me come
   From music that was mine,
The songs of sweetest birds at home,
   Of holy clerks at shrine :
From men of gentle courtesie,
   Of stately strength and air,
And ladies of all dames that be
   Most worshipful and fair !

IV

Albyn the cold and fierce and wild,
   Land of disease and crime,
Land of the naked and defiled,
   Be thou my chosen clime !
But, Erin, seven times for thy sake
   My pleadings seek the sky ;—
Ah, 'twill be, if my heartstrings break,
   For love of thee I die !

PARAPHRASE IN ENGLISH

FROM THE LATIN OF THE

(I)   'ALTUS PROSATOR'

AND

(II) 'IN TE, CHRISTE, CREDENTIUM'

REPUTED HYMNS OF ST. COLUMBA

WITH NOTES, ETC.

THE following notes are, for the most part, a summary of those given in the edition of *The Book of Hymns of the Irish Church* (Fasciculus II.): edited for the Irish Archæological and Celtic Society by Dr. J. H. Todd (Dublin, 1869). The author of this Paraphrase acknowledges gratefully the help he has had from this work.

1. The Hymn was first printed by Colgan from an ancient copy of the *Book of Hymns*, supposed to be that which is now in St. Isidore's at Rome. The text is in many places corrupt, arising from errors of the press or of transcription.

2. Two accounts are given of its composition: one, that it was a penitential exercise written by St. Columba after years of study (before his mission to Iona), in the Black Church of Derry in Ireland, because of the battles in which he had had part;— the second, that it was uttered extemporaneously in

Hy (Iona) on the occasion of the visit of certain messengers from Rome sent by Gregory the Great. The former account of its origin is very much the more probable. Any such mission, if it had taken place, would have been recorded by Adamnan.

3. That the Hymn is not mentioned by Adamnan is no argument against its authenticity, because the plan of his work did not necessarily involve any notice of the writings of St. Columba.

4. The Hymn is written in a rude Latinity; each strophe of six double lines beginning with a special letter of the alphabet in order. The metre is a species of Trochaic Dimeter with a rhyme or, rather, assonance in the middle and at the end of each line of sixteen syllables : *e.g.*—

Salva fide in Personis Tribus gloriosissimis,

otherwise printed (to show the assonance) in double lines of eight syllables—

Salva fide in Personis
Tribus gloriosissimis.

(*N.B.*—The English translation, or Paraphrase, in verse in the following pages, has been made so as to follow the break of the double line indicated by the rhyme or assonance.)

5. In the old MS. a Scholium is prefixed to each strophe or stanza, containing 'The Title' and 'The Argument.' The *Title* is a short summary of the subject treated of.

The *Argument* is one or more texts of Scripture indicating the principal thought or subject-matter of the stanza. The glosses are many, and often of interest and value.

6. Even those who are inclined to be sceptical as to the authorship cannot have a doubt of the great antiquity of the Hymn.

It quotes in many places a Latin version of the Scriptures older than the recension of St. Jerome, and it is written in a barbaric style, with many words of rare occurrence, and some unknown to the Dictionaries; and occasionally grammatical liberties are taken for sake of metre or rhyme.

7. In relation to the *Vetustus Dierum*, 'Ancient of Days,' in the first line of *Capitulum A*, it is interesting to note what the Scholiast says of the Argument: 'It is the canon (*i.e.* text) on which the Capitulum (*i.e.* stanza) is founded, as it is read in Daniel vii. 9

or in Isaias vi. : Columcille (*i.e.* Columba) gives in it the canon of a prophet because he (*i.e.* Columba) was a Prophet ; and it is chiefly from Daniel that he takes it, because he was the latest and noblest : and Columcille was the latest and noblest of the Prophets of Erin.'

(*N.B.* ii.—Every strophe or stanza throughout the Hymn has six lines (in full length), or twelve lines (divided at the assonance), *except the first*, Capitulum A.   This has seven double lines or fourteen single.

The object of this difference has been variously explained, in the Preface to the *Leabhar Breac* (which is a mixture of Latin and Gaelic), in the following way :—'Now there are six lines in every Capitulum except the first Capitulum, and sixteen syllables in every line; and seven lines in the first Capitulum. It is fit that there should be six lines where is narrated all that was finished in six days.   And it is fit that there should be seven lines in the first Capitulum, because it tells of GOD, for GOD is not comparable to His creatures; or it signifies the seven grades of the Church; or that the number seven denotes universality; or it signifies the seven gifts of the HOLY GHOST.')

CAPITULUM A

ALTUS prosator vetustus
dierum et ingenitus
erat absque origine
primordii et crepidine
est et erit in secula
seculorum infinita
cui est unigenitus
christus et sanctus spiritus
coeternus in gloria
dietatis perpetuae
non tris deos depromimus
sed unum deum dicimus
salva fide in personis
tribus gloriosissimis.

STANZA A

TITLE: *De unitate et Trinitate trium personarum.*
ARGUMENT: ' *Vetustus dierum sedebat super sedem suam.*'
(DANIEL vii. 9.)

HIGH CREATOR, Unbegotten,
    Ancient of Eternal days,
Unbegun ere all beginning,
    Him, the world's one source, we praise:
GOD who is, and GOD who shall be:
    All that was and is before:
Him with CHRIST the Sole-Begotten,
    And the SPIRIT we adore,
Co-eternal, one in glory,
    Evermore and evermore:—
Not Three Gods are They we worship,
    But the THREE which are the ONE,
GOD, in Three most glorious Persons:—
    Other saving Faith is none.

Bonos creavit angelos
ordines et archangelos
principatuum ac sedium
potestatum virtutium
uti non esset bonitas
otiosa ac maiestas
trinitatis in omnibus
largitatis muneribus
sed haberet celestia
in quibus previgilia
ostenderet magnopere
possibili fatimine.

STANZA B

TITLE: *De formatione novem graduum*, tribus praetermissis, non per ignorantiam, sed pro augustia capituli praetermisit.
ARGUMENT: '*Fiat lux*, *et facta est*.'

ALL good angels and archangels,
    Powers and Principalities,
Virtues, Thrones, His will created—
    Grades and orders of the skies,
That the majesty and goodness
    Of the Blessed TRINITY
In its ever bounteous largesse
    Never might inactive be;
Having thus wherewith to glory,
    All the wide world might adore
The high Godhead's sole-possession
    Everywhere and evermore.

CAPITULUM C

Celi de regni apice
stationis angelicae
claritate prefulgoris
venustate speciminis
superbiendo ruerat
lucifer quem formaverat
apostataeque angeli
eodem lapsu lugubri
auctoris ceno-doxiae
pervicacis invidiae
ceteris remanentibus
in suis principatibus.

STANZA C

Title : *De transmigratione novem graduum principis.*
Argument : '*Vidi stellam de cœlo cecidisse in terram*'; et in
Esaiâ, '*Quomodo cecidisti Lucifer, qui mane oriebaris.*'

Prone, from splendour of that kingdom
   Where God's angels crown the height,
From all loveliness of beauty
   All transcendency of light,
Lucifer, by God created,
   Fell by his vainglorious pride—
Fell by envy still persisting,
   Fell with all his host allied,
From the same high place apostate
   In the same sad ruin prone,—
While the faithful angel princes
   Kept their state before the Throne.

CAPITULUM D

Draco magnus deterrimus
terribilis et antiquus
qui fuit serpens lubricus
sapientior omnibus
bestiis et animantibus
terrae feracioribus
tertiam partem siderum
traxit secum in barathrum
locorum infernalium
diversorumque carcerum
refuga veri luminis
parasito praecipites.

STANZA D

TITLE : *De ruina Diaboli, i.e. De mutatione nominis Luciferi in Draconem.*

ARGUMENT : '*Ecce Draco Rufus habens capita septem, et cornua decem, et cauda ejus traxit secum tertiam partem siderum vel stellarum.*'—(APOC. xii. 3.)

THE old Dragon, loathliest, fiercest,
    Serpent shrewdest in all guile
And more dread than all the creatures
    That devour man or defile,
Down with him drew headlong—falling
    From the heavenly spaces far
Of the highest constellations—
    All the third part, star by star,
Headlong—to the depths infernal,
    All the diverse cells of night :
Headlong fell each doomed apostate
    From the Paradise of light.

CAPITULUM E

EXCELSUS mundi machinam
previdens et armoniam
caelum et terram fecerat
mare et aquas condidit
herbarum quoque germina
virgultorum arbuscula
solem lunam ac sidera
ignem ac necessaria
aves pisces et peccora
bestias et animalia
hominum demum regere
protoplastum praesagmine.

STANZA E

TITLE : *De creatione elementorum mundi et hominis regentis ca postea more regis.*

ARGUMENT : '*In principio fecit Deus celum et terram*' *ut in Genesi dicitur.*—(GEN. i. 1.)

God, the Lord Most High, foreseeing
    Nature's concord full and sweet,
Moulded Heaven and Earth and Ocean
    To one harmony complete :
Sprang the grasses, fair unfolding,
    Copses burgeoned in the sun :
Beamed the sunlight, starlight, moonlight,
    Firelight : all of need was done—
Birds for brake, and fish for waters,
    Wild or tame kine for the sward—
Last, the highest, first created,
    Man, Creation's crown and lord.

CAPITULUM F

FACTIS simul sideribus
etheris luminaribus
collaudaverunt angeli
factura praemirabili
immensae molis dominum
opificem celestium
preconia laudabile
debito et immobile
concentuque egregio
grates egerunt domino
amore et arbitrio
non naturae donario.

STANZA F

WHEN together, æther's wonder,
    Shine the Stars, the Angels sing ;
To th' Immensity's Designer,
    Host on host, their anthems ring :
Songs right meet for adoration,
    Glorious harmonies they raise ;
Since they move not from their courses
    Never-ending is their praise.
Noble concert in the highest
    Is their offering full and free :—
'Tis of love's sincerest rapture
    Not of natural decree.

Grassatis primis duobus
seductisque parentibus
secundo ruit zabulus
cum suis satilitibus
quorum horrore vultuum
sonoque volitantium
consternarentur homines
metu territi fragiles
non valentes carnalibus
haec intueri visibus
qui nunc ligantur fascibus
ergastolorum nexibus.

STANZA G

TITLE: *De peccato Adae et de secunda ruina Diaboli in seductione Adae.*

ARGUMENT: '*Maledictus eris serpens, terram comederis omnibus diebus vitae.*'—(GEN. iii. 14.)

WHEN beneath the lord of evil
    Fell the parents of our race—
By his guile assailed and ruined—
    From their purity and grace,
Then their foeman and his legions
    Fell too by a second fall,
And the hopeless realms infernal
    Hold them bound in spirit thrall,
Lest—such dread forms on their vision,
    And such wild wings on their ear—
Weak and frail souls should be stricken
    With intolerable fear.

CAPITULUM H

Hɪc sublatus e medio
dejectus est a domino
cujus aeris spatium
constipatur satilitum
globo invisibilium
turbido perduellium
ne malis exemplaribus
imbuti ac sceleribus
nullis unquam tegentibus
septis ac parietibus
fornicarentur homines
palam omnium oculis.

TITLE : *De ejectione Diabuli e communitate Angelorum.*
ARGUMENT : '*Maledicte serpens*' (GENESIS), and in the Gospel it
is said '*Vade retro, Satanas*' (ST. MATT. iv. 10), '*et non temptabis
Dominum Deum tuum et illi soli servies.*'—(ST. MATT. iv. 7.)

FROM the midst of sinless angels
    Lo, the LORD hath cast him down !
Filled are all th' aërial spaces
    With his legions overthrown,
Viewless all, lest foul example—
    Vision of alluring fiend—
Should avail for man's seduction,
    By no prison barrier screened :
Lest the vision of the rebel
    Should seduce the leal and true,
And such open foul misdoing
    Should the purest lives undo.

K

Invehunt nubes pontias
ex fontibus brumalias
tribus profundioribus
occiani dodrantibus
maris celi climatibus
ceruleis turbinibus
profuturas segitibus
viniis et germinibus
agitatae flaminibus
tesauris emergentibus
quique paludes marinas
evacuant reciprocas.

STANZA I

TITLE : *De eo quod vehunt nubes aquas ad cœlum.*
ARGUMENT : As David says : ' *Educens nubes ab extremo terrae* ;
and ' *Qui produxit ventos de thesauris tuis.*'—(PS. cxxxv. 7.)

FROM the three deep tracts of ocean,
On the blue sky's rushing wings,
Clouds convey the floods of winter
Upward from the parent springs,
On to every clime of heaven
By the strong winds urged amain,
As they quit their houses laden
With the treasures of the rain :—
Floods which feed the crops and vineyards
And the buds of plant and tree :—
Winds which ever, morn and even,
Drain the deep pools of the sea.

CAPITULUM K

KADUCA ac tirannica
mundique momentania
regum presenti gloria
nutu dei deposita
ecce gigantes gemere
sub aquis magno ulcere
comprobantur incendio
aduri ac suplicio
cocitique carubdibus
strangulati turgentibus
scillis obtecti fluctibus
eliduntur et scropibus.

STANZA K

Title : *De intolerabili poena peccatorum.*
Argument : Quod Job dicit : ' *Ecce gigantes gemunt sub aquis.*'
(Job xxvi. 5.)

By God's will the Tyrant's glories—
    Tottering splendours of the world,
Pride of kings—as in a moment,
    Are in ruin overhurled ;
Yonder see the giants ancient
    By a doom which none arraign
Groan beneath the whelming waters
    Of intolerable pain :
Or they agonise for ever
    Where the burning fiery grave,
Or Hell's Scylla and Charybdis,
    Are their ruin,—rock and wave.

CAPITULUM L

Ligatas aquas nubibus
frequenter crebrat dominus
ut ne erumpant protinus
simul ruptis obiicibus
quarum uberioribus
venis velut uberibus
pedetemtim natantibus
telli pertractus istius
gellidis ac ferventibus
diversis in temporibus
usquam influunt flumina
nunquam deficientia.

STANZA L

TITLE: *De moderatione fluviae venientis ex ligatis aquis nubibus ne pariter fluant.*

ARGUMENT: Quod Job dicit: '*Qui suspendit aquas in nubibus ne pariter fluant deorsum.*'—(JOB xxvi. 8.)

FROM the LORD the rain's soft showerings
    Ever fall at need below:
Closely stored behind their barriers
    Lest their bounty overflow:
Slowly, surely fertilising,
    Never failing at His will,
They as if from breast maternal
    O'er the earth their balm distil:
So the rivers in their season,
    From the winter to the spring,
To the autumn from the summer
    Their inflowings ever bring.

CAPITULUM M

Magno dei virtutibus
appenditur dialibus
globus terrae et circulus
abyssi magnae inditus
suffulta dei iduma
omnipotentis valida
columnis velut vectibus
eundem sustentantibus
promontoriis et rupibus
solidis fundaminibus
velut quibusdam bassibus
firmatis immobilibus.

STANZA M

Title : *De fundamento terrae et de abisso.*
Argument : '*Qui suspendit terram (super nihilum.*')—(Job xxvi.
7.) Et alibi : ' *Moles mundi virtute Dei continetur.*' Et in Psalmo
' *Qui fundasti terram super stabilitatem suam.*'

This great globe doth God the Highest
  By His power all surely keep :
And the fixed unchanging circle
  Of the dread abysmal deep.
Firm, as on sustaining columns,
  Did the mighty orb arise,
His strong hand the mass upholding,
  Lo, the pillared structure lies ;
Heights and bases of the mountains
  Rise and rest beneath His Hands :
On immovable foundations
  The eternal structure stands.

Nulli videtur dubium
in imis esse infernum
ubi habentur tenebrae
vermes ac dirae bestiae
ubi ignis solphorius
ardens flammis edacibus
ubi rugitus hominum
fletus ac stridor dentium
ubi gehennae gemitus
terribilis et antiquus
ubi ardor flammaticus
sitis famisque horridus.

TITLE: *De inferno in imis posito in corde terrae et poenis ejus et loco.*

ARGUMENT: '*Eruisti animam meam ex inferno inferiori.*' '*Sepultus est dives in inferno.*'—(ST. LUKE xvi. 22.) '*Ite, maledicti in eternum ignem.*'—(ST. MATT. xxv. 41.) '*Vermis eorum non moritur et ignis ejus non extinguitur.*'—(ST. MARK ix. 48.)

HAUNT the realms of gloom infernal
    (Dread this truth that none deny!)
Crawling worm and loathly creature
    Where the depths profoundest lie.
There the sulphurous fire for ever
    Blazes with consuming flame:
There is heard in wail and weeping
    Every sound of woe and shame:
There the horror of Gehenna
    Is perpetual as dire:
There in pangs of thirst and famine
    Burns a never-ceasing fire.

CAPITULUM O

ORBEM infra ut legimus
incolas esse novimus
quorum genu praecario
frequenter flectit domino
quibusque impossibili
librum scriptum revolvere
obsignatum signaculis
. . . . monitis
quem idem resignaverat
per quem victor extiterat
explens sui praesagmina
adventus prophetalia.

STANZA O

TITLE : *Of the inhabitants of Hell who for very shame bow down in the name of the Lord.*

ARGUMENT : ' *Donavit Illi nomen quod est super omne nomen.*'

(Ph. ii. 9.)

READ we that in mystic regions,
　　Far below this earthly floor,
There are dwellers in the darkness
　　Who the One Great Name adore :
That they failed before the bidding
　　When the Book, the seven-sealed,
Lay before them for unrolling,
　　But still lay there unrevealed :
Till the Slain Lamb, now the Victor,
　　Laid it bare to every eye ;
Of His Advent thus fulfilling
　　All the old prophetic cry.

CAPITULUM P

Plantatum a prohemio
paradisum a domino
legimus in primordio
genesis nobilissimo
cujus ex fonte flumina
quatuor sunt manantia
cujus ex situm florido
lignum vitae est medio
cujus non cadunt folia
gentibus salutifera
cujus inenarrabiles
deliciae ac fertiles.

STANZA P

TITLE: *De Paradiso Adae, id est, loco deliciarum.*
ARGUMENT: '*Plantaverat Paradisum voluptatis a principio.*'
(GEN. ii. 8.)   Also APOC. ii. 7, and APOC. xxii. 2.

IN the Holy Word's beginning
　　Nobly writ for reverent eyes,
Learn we by GOD's Hand was planted
　　Blest primordial Paradise:
From its fountain the four Rivers
　　Through the meads rejoicing flow,
In the midst—Life's Tree encircling—
　　Sweetest flowers of beauty blow;
Never fail its leaves of healing
　　For the wide world far away;
How delightsome are its pleasures
　　None may measure, none may say.

CAPITULUM Q

Quis ad condictum domini
montem conscendit sinai
quis audivit tonitrua
supra modum sonantia
quis clangorem perstreperae
enormitatis buccinae
quis quoque vidit fulgura
in gyro coruscantia
quis lampades et jacula
saxaque collidentia
praeter israelitici
moysem judicem populi.

STANZA Q

TITLE : *De ascensione Moysis ad Dominum in Monte Sinai.*
(EXOD. xxiv. 15, 16.)
ARGUMENT : '*Facta sunt tonitrua et voces et fulgura et terrae
motus.*'—(APOC. xvi. 18.)

WHO that height by GOD appointed,
 Sinai, hath essayed and found ?
Who hath heard the thunders hurtling
 With immeasurable sound ?
Who th' enormous trumpet blaring,
 With the silences between ?
Who the lightning's flashes, piercing
 All the thickest dark, hath seen ?
Who hath witnessed rocks down crashing,
 Lamp that gleamed and dart that fell ?
None hath heard or seen but Moses,
 Judge and Prince of Israel.

L

CAPITULUM R

REGIS regum rectissimi
prope est dies domini
dies irae et vindictae
tenebrarum et nebulae
diesque mirabilium
tonitruorum fortium
dies quoque angustiae
moeroris ac tristitiae
in quo cessabit mulierum
amor et desiderium
hominumque contentio
mundi hujus et cupido.

STANZA R

TITLE : *De Die judicii et nominibus ejus.*
ARGUMENT : '*Juxta est Dies Domini magnus et velox nimis.*'
(ZEPH. i. 14-16.)

OF the King of kings, most Righteous,
   Lo, the last dread day is near !
'Tis the day of cloud and darkness,
   Day of vengeance, day of fear ;
Hear the voice of the strong thunders,
   Rolling on the shuddering air,
Heralding the day of terror,
   Day of mourning and despair !
Now no more the love of women,
   Or men's strife in passion hurled !
Now no more the rage of battle,
   Or the fierce lusts of the world !

CAPITULUM S

STANTES erimus pavidi
ante tribunal domini
reddemusque de omnibus
rationem effectibus
videntes quoque posita
ante obtutus crimina
librosque conscientiac
patefactos in facie
in fletus amarissimos
ac singultus erumpemus
subtracta necessaria
operandi materia.

STANZA S

TITLE : *De tremebunda praesentiâ Dei in die judicii.*
ARGUMENT : '*Oportet nos omnes stare ante Tribunal Christi.*'
(2 COR. v. 10), and ST. MATT. xvi. 27.

AT the LORD's tribunal trembling,
   For just judgment we shall stand ;
For each act its own due motive—
   For each word—He will demand :
Of all ill each word and action
   Long concealed shall face the sight :
Books of conscience long in hiding
   Shall lie open to the light ;
Oh, the weeping, the wild weeping !
   Oh, the bitterness that scars !
Place is none now for repentance,
   Place is none for work or tears.

CAPITULUM T

Tuba prima archangeli
strepente admirabilia
erumpent munitissima
claustra ac poliandria
mundi praesentis frigora
hominum liquescentia
undique conglobantibus
ad compagines ossibus
animabus aetherialibus
eisdem obeuntibus
rursumque redeuntibus
debitis in mansionibus.

STANZA T

TITLE: *De Resurrectione prolis Adac.*
ARGUMENT: '*Ipse Dominus ut in jussu et in voce Archangeli in tuba descendet de celo.*'—(1 THESS. iv. 16), and APOC. x. 7.

WHEN the trump of the archangel
  Pealeth wondrous loud and long,
Is there tomb too barred for breaking?
  Is there cloister wall too strong?
Then shall melt before its summons
  The death-frozen heart of man,
See the bones that time hath scattered
  Portioned by their ancient plan!
From afar the soul ethereal
  In the flesh returns to reign:
And the old deserted mansions
  Now receive their own again.

N.B.—Capitulum U in Colgan's Edition is too corrupt for attempt at translation.

CAPITULUM X

Xto de coelis domino
descendente altissimo
praefulgebit clarissimum
signum crucis et vexillum
tactisque luminaribus
duobus principalibus
cadent in terram sydera
ut fructus de ficulnea
eritque mundi spatium
ut fornacis incendium
tunc in montium specubus
abscondent se exercitus.

STANZA X

TITLE : *De Die judici et praefulgente ligno Crucis.*

ARGUMENT : '*Abscondent se in speluncis et petris montium et tunc dicent montibus super nos cadite.*'—(APOC. vi. 15, 16), and ST. MATT. xxiv. 29.

WHEN from Heaven to Earth descending
    Comes the CHRIST in power divine,
Then the Signal Cross, His Banner,
    Shall all gloriously shine ;
Then the lords of light before Him,
    Sun and moon, shall shrink and pale,
And the stars, like fruit untimely
    From the wind-wrecked tree, shall fail.
As the burning of a furnace
    See the whole vast world appear,
All its hosts in mountain caverns
    Hide their heads in mortal fear.

Ymnorum cantionibus
sedulo tinnientibus
tropodis sanctis milibus
angelorum vernantibus
quatuorque plenissimis
animalibus oculis
cum viginti felicibus
quatuor senioribus
coronas admittentibus
agni dei sub pedibus
laudatur tribus vicibus
trinitas eternalibus.

STANZA V

TITLE : *De laude Dei ab angelis.*
ARGUMENT : '*In circuitu throni vidi sedes xxiv. seniores sedentes in veste alba et capitibus eorum corona aurea vidi.*'—(APOC. iv. 4.)

HYMNS are chanted, sweetly measured,
    Evermore and evermore,
To the rhythmic feet of angels
    On the heavenly golden floor ;
And the four great Living Creatures
    With their myriad eyes of light,
And the four-and-twenty Elders
    Crowned with gold and robed in white,
There before the LAMB adoring
    Cast their crowns upon the sea,
'Sanctus, Sanctus, Sanctus,' singing
    To th' adorèd TRINITY.

Zelus ignis furibundus
consumet adversarios
nolentes christum credere
deo a patre venisse
nos vero evolabimus
obviam ei protinus
et sic cum ipso erimus
in diversis ordinibus
dignitatum pro meritis
premiorum perpetuis
permansuri in gloria
a seculis in gloria.

STANZA Z

TITLE: *De ustione malorum nolentes* (sic) *Christum credere et de gaudio justorum.'*
ARGUMENT: ' *Terribilis ignis consumet adversarios.'*
(HEB. x. 27), and ST. JOHN xiv. 3.

FIRE of wrath shall be the portion
   Of apostates who deny
That the CHRIST came from the FATHER,
   Very GOD of GOD Most High;
But the Saints go forth to meet Him—
   Fly to meet Him in the air—
Each one in his rank and order
   Shall one happy guerdon share;
Each shall have his fitting portion,
   And, for endless high reward,
Shall in glory be for ever
   And for ever with the LORD.

Amen.

ANTIPHON

Quis potest deo placere
novissimo in tempore
variatis insignibus
veritatis ordinibus
exceptis contemptoribus
mundi presentis istius.

ANTIPHON

Deum patrem ingenitum
coeli ac terrae dominum
ab eodemque filium
secula ante primogenitum
deumque spiritum sanctum
verum unum altissimum
invoco ut auxillium
mihi opportunissimum
minimo prestet omnium
sibi deservientium
quem angelorum[1] millibus
consociabit dominus.

[1] S. Mark xii. 25.

ANTIPHON

Now the times are near their ending,
    Who may hope to please his LORD,
Since the notes of Truth are parted
    From their old divine accord?—
Only they, this world despising,
    Who in heart to heaven have soared.

ANTIPHON

THEE, the FATHER, unbegotten,
    Only LORD of Heaven and Earth :
Thee, from Him, the One Begotten
    By the one Eternal Birth :
Thee the SPIRIT, Holiest, Highest,
    GOD of Unity and Truth,
I invoke—for mine inspiring,
    For mine aid in very sooth :
Mine—though I, of all who follow,
    Hold the lowest, meanest place :
Even me my LORD will number
    With His blest ones by His grace.
               Amen.

THE HYMN

In Te, Christe

In te christe credentium
miserearis omnium
tu es deus in secula
seculorum in gloria

Deus in adiutorium
intende laborantium
ad dolorum remedium
festina in auxillium

Deus pater credentium
deus vita viventium
deus deorum omnium
deus virtus virtutium

Deus formator omnium
deus et judex judicum
deus et princeps principum
elimentorum omnium

Christ, to us in Thee believing
   Grant Thy mercy, we implore,
Who art God from all the ages
   To the ages evermore.

God, be Thou our strength and succour,
   Labouring all the weary day:
Haste in all our hours of sorrow
   To be all our hope and stay.

God, the Father of believers,
   God, the life of all who live;
God of gods, Who dost to virtue
   All the soul of virtue give.

God, of all things Sole Creator,
   Of all judges Judge alone:
Prince of all the princes ruling
   On each elemental throne.

M

Deus opis eximiae
celestis hierusolimae
deus rex regni in gloria
deus ipse viventium

Deus aeterni luminis
deus inenarrabilis
deus altus amabilis
deus inestimabilis

Deus largus longanimis
deus doctor docibilis
deus qui facit omnia
nova cuncta et vetera

Dei patris in nomine
filique sui prospere
sancti spiritus utique
recto vado itinere

Christus redemptor gentium
christus amator virginum
christus fons sapientium
christus fides credentium

GOD of every help the surest,
  GOD of Salem's blest abode :
GOD of all the realms of glory,—
  Of the Quick the living GOD ;

GOD of Light the Everlasting :
  GOD Whose record none can tell ;
GOD the lofty and the loving,
  Who dost, past all praise, excel.

GOD, long-suffering in Thy greatness,
  Of Thy learners Teacher true :
Thou art GOD, the only Maker
  Of the ancient and the new.

In the Name of GOD the FATHER,
  Of the SPIRIT, and the SON—
Thus I go my way with blessing,
  Other path to life is none.

CHRIST, Redeemer of the nations,
  CHRIST the lover of the pure,
CHRIST the fountain of all wisdom,
  Of all Faith the founder sure.

Christus lorica militum
christus creator omnium
christus salus viventium
et vita morientium

Coronavit exercitum
nostrum cum turba martirum
christus crucem ascenderat
christus mundum salvaverat

Christus et nos redemerat
christus pro nobis passus est
christus cum deo sederat
ubi numquam defuerat

Gloria haec est altissimo
deo patri ingenito
honor ac sumno filio
unico unigenito

Spirituique obtimo
sancto perfecto sedulo
amen fiat perpetua
In sempiterna secula

In te, etc.

CHRIST, of all who war, the Breastplate,
   CHRIST the source of earth and sky,
CHRIST the Saviour of the living,
   And the life of all who die.

He has crowned our noble army
   With His martyrs' glorious host,
He the altar Cross ascended,
   Only Saviour of the lost.

CHRIST is He Who has redeemed us,
   CHRIST Who for our sins atoned,
Yet was throned with GOD the FATHER,
   And from Godhead ne'er dethroned.

To the FATHER Unbegotten,
   To the Sole-begotten SON,
Highest, greatest—be this honour,
   This our glorying, duly done :—

And to Him, Best SPIRIT Holy,
   Ceaseless let our praises be :
While the ages everlasting
   Say Amen eternally !

                      Amen.

ST. COLUMB OF IONA

A LAY OF THE 'FAMILY OF HY'

St. Columb of Iona: a Lay[1] of the 'Family of Hy'

I

Iona's hills are lowly,
    Her rocks are bleak and wild,
Frowns Mull the mighty o'er her
    As at a changeling child ;
O'er the dividing waters
    She sends no mother's smile :
No kin the granite giant
    Owns in the darker isle.

II

Iona sends for pleading
    No suit of tender grace :
No fee of form majestic,
    No wile of winsome face :—
No forests make her stately,
    No rivers make her fair,
She lieth still o'er vale and hill,
    As if in meek despair.

[1] See Preface, p. xvi.

III

Yet hath the Lord from Heaven
   Looked on the lowly isle;
His promise shall not tarry,
   The wilderness shall smile,
And, on these bleak rocks, beautiful
   Shall be their feet who stand—
The heralds of that Lord of Love
   Who died in Holy Land.

IV

But long years—half a thousand—
   Have fled in weary line,
And nought hath waked the silence,
   And none hath seen a sign;
By feet that bring no blessing
   Iona still is trod;
And priests unknown of Sion
   Worship an unknown God.[1]

V

The ocean winds that sweep her
   Breathe sadness still in tone,

---

[1] The Druids acknowledged only one God.

The ocean voice rolls round her
As one that maketh moan ;
For, from the chosen island,
In tempest or in calm,
Rises in air, for praise or prayer,
Nor litany nor psalm.

VI

But now ! the burden changeth,
Though none the change may know,
Save those who joy in heaven
For blessing wrought below ;
The mournful burden changeth,
Like weeping into song ;
Like those who cry, ' He cometh ! '
Who wailed before, ' How long ? '

VII

'Tis on a silent even,
After the glare of day,
A frail boat to Iona
Is wending peaceful way ;
A glow is on the waters,
A charm is in the air,

And the blessing Pentecostal [1]
Seems falling everywhere.

VIII

Long was the weary waiting,
　The desolate day was long,
But peace has come at sunset,
　Like praise at evensong !
Cometh Iona's promise,
　In that frail boat on the sea,
As of old the Hope of a world forlorn,
The future Church and her LORD, was borne
　On the waves of Galilee !

IX

A saint and his twelve companions
　Are all the waters bear ;
They wave no warring standard,
　No battle-arms they bear :
CHRIST'S Cross their warrior token ;
　His Word the sword they wield ;
But whose are brand and banner
　So blest on foughten field ?

---

[1] It was on the evening before Whitsunday that St. Columba arrived first
at Iona. (See Note 3, p. 35.)

X

St. Columb's name is noble,
  Of kingly line is he;
And rich broad lands and vassal bands
  Are his in his own countrie.
But homage, and wealth, and sceptre,
  He lays right gladly down;
Who counts the Cross his glory
  Recks not of fleeting crown!

XI

Priests of the old delusion,
  Fear for your ancient reign!
A mightier than the Roman
  Here cometh o'er the main:
Soon shall the Golden Sickle
  Gleam in the oak no more;
No more the stones of the cromlech
  Be red with human gore.
The charm of your day is passing,
  A new strange 'fire of God'[1]
Shall wither the worn-out tokens,
  The Amulet and the Rod:

[1] The great Druidical festival took place in May, and was called the Feast of the 'Fire of God,' in honour of the sun.

There shall rise a temple stately
For every shapeless shrine,
And a threefold priestly order
Supplant your triple line ![1]

XII

Now be she named Ishona !
Now call her Holy Isle ![2]
Now may the winds be jocund,
Now may the waters smile !
For proud at the sacred service
They render the freight they bore,
As the saints of the great Redeemer
Stand on the chosen shore.

XIII

He calls his Twelve around him,
As a chieftain calls his clan,
For zealous deed in some sore need
Exhorting every man :
' Behold,' he saith, ' the darkness
Deep o'er the northern land !

[1] There were three orders or grades among the Druids : the Druids proper, the Bards, and the Vates.
[2] The Gaelic *Ishona* signifies Holy Island.

And ye, the Sons of Morning,
   To shine at the LORD's command !
Shine ye forth at His bidding,
   O new, best light of souls,
Till from the chosen kingdom
   The death-shade backward rolls !

XIV

'Far are ye from the borders
   The feet of JESUS trod,
Far from the Holy City,
   Far from the Hill of God :
But the Pentecostal Presence
   Is brooding everywhere,
And the whole earth is Sion,
   And JESUS reigneth there !
To every wind of heaven
   His standard is outfurled,
His kingdom's only limit
   The kingdoms of the world !

XV

'Scatter the ancient shadows,
   Grace of the mystic TRINE !

O Human tender pity,
  O love and power Divine !
Gather the northern peoples,
  Gather them near and far,
To follow the herald promise
  Of the Western morning star.'[1]

XVI

The saint fulfils his praying—
  Whose life is as his prayer
Shall work the work he willeth,
  And safely do and dare :
The LORD GOD is his keeper,
  And His strong angels stand
To watch and ward, to guide and guard
  Ever on either hand.

XVII

King Brude [2] is lord of Pictland :
  Fierce is his heart and hard,
And fast against the stranger
  His castle gate is barred ;

---

[1] An expression applied frequently to Iona.

[2] Brude or Brudius (or Bruti), king of the Picts, who was subsequently his warm friend, at first shut his gates upon him.

But, as the gentle sea-tide
  O'erflows the rugged shore,
Ere long the saintly spirit
  Winneth the proud heart o'er!

XVIII

Fell is his foemen's malice,
  More fell the Druid's wile;
But neither threat may daunt him,
  Nor treachery beguile.
Through pain, and toil, and vigil
  Ever so passeth he,
With a steadfast heart through every one,
As of old through the fire in Babylon
  Did pass the holy Three.

XIX

As after hours of tempest,
  Or ere the day be done,
Pierces the rolling cloud-rack
  The great orb of the sun;
And all the broken heaven,
  And the waste world below,
Is bathed with his tender glory,
  A deeper golden glow;—

N

XX

So to the heathen peoples,
  As after gloom of storm,
With light of the great evangel
  Stands forth St. Columb's form :
Outpouring peace on hatred,
  And closing years of strife ;
Like a visible benediction
  Outbreathing a new life.

XXI

Behold they throng around him !
  Vassals, and chiefs, and kings ;
From the poet-lips [1] that scorned him
  His fame and honour rings.
See how the wild barbarians
  Kneel at his loving word,
And come, like sheep that have wandered,
  Back to the Shepherd-lord !

XXII

Fear is in his rebuking,
  Strength in his clear command,

---

1 The bards, at first his bitterest foes, ultimately became most friendly
and sang his praises.

But Love in his long forbearing,
  And Blessing beneath his hand:
Tenderly loosing the burden,
  Yet crushing the pride of sin,
He bringeth the fierce with the fearful,
  The stern with the gentle, in!

XXIII

Conqueror, true and noble!
  Not now the wasted lands,
Not now the riven banner
  And reeking battle brands!
But a kingdom torn from Satan,
  And the spoil of souls unpriced,
Won painfully, laid humbly
  At the feet of the Lord CHRIST!

XXIV

Won painfully—in vigils,
  In labours night and day,
Preparing in the desert
  The coming King's highway:

Laid humbly—with no vaunting,
But meekly as by one
Counting his hands not worthy
To loose the Master's shoon.

XXV

See, high in barren places,
Springs hallowed house, or shrine—
Of unseen spirit-blessing
The visible fair sign-—
And winds, that breathed the rancour
Of human hate and wrong,
Bear now the heavenly incense
Of morn and even-song.

XXVI

Praise to the LORD of harvest!
The waste land is a field
Wherein the sower's labour
A hundredfold doth yield:
Seed which the SPIRIT wafteth
Far on from clime to clime,
To be reaped at last by the angels,
At blessed Harvest-time.

XXVII

But he dies—the saintly sower—
  Lo, 'tis the Eve of Morn : [1]
With joyful praise he seeth
  The garnered wealth of corn ;
'They shall not lack,' he crieth,
  'The children shall be blest,
Though the long Sabbath calleth
  The father unto rest !'

XXVIII

Now o'er the sacred College
  On the Torr Abb he stands,
And prophet-benediction
  Falls from his lifted hands :
'Lo, great shall be thy triumph
  O'er evil overhurled !
And thou, the meek and poor, be found
Chosen and precious, when thy sound
  Is heard in all the world.'

---

[1] On the morning of Saturday, the day before he died, he visited the granary of the monastery, and gave thanks for the provision for the sustenance of those whom he was about to leave.

XXIX

Now, 'tis the hour of vigil—
　　The father in his cell
Hears on the air the call for prayer
　　Ring from the midnight bell.
Long ere the monks have risen
　　His feet have passed the door,
And at the Altar lowly
　　He kneeleth on the floor.

XXX

'Where art thou, O my father?'
　　One crieth through the gloom :[1]
But the darkness is as silent
　　As the darkness of the tomb.
With haste they bring the tapers,
　　With fear they gather round ;
But in answer to their crying
　　Is neither sign nor sound.

XXXI

Then gently they uplift him,
　　And lo !—a little space—

---

[1] Dermid, the monk who was his continual attendant.

An infinite sweet rapture
  Doth lighten in his face;
And well they knew he seeth
  The heralds of Reward!
The guardians of the blessèd,
  The liegemen of the LORD!

XXXII

Yet once he turneth on them
  One last long look of love;
One moment, for last blessing,
  They raise his hand above;
And then they watch him wildly,
  And then they turn and weep—
The soul hath passed to Eden,
  The body into sleep.

XXXIII

Iona! Holy island!
  Isle of St. Columb's cell![1]
The very names thou bearest
  Love all thy children well.
Ringed by thy rainbow waters,
  Crowned by thy peerless skies,

[1] Icolmkill is the form in which this title of the Island is still retained.

Where change on change unchanging
  For ever lives and dies :
To us thy thought is dearer
  Than of all lovely lands,
With all their lordly mountains,
  And all their golden sands.

XXXIV

What say our seers ?[1]   Hereafter
  When storm shall shake the world,
And in one vast sea-ruin
  Nations are overhurled—
When Erin lies and Islay
  'Neath the sepulchral wave,
And of the hundred islands
  Each finds its own sea-grave ;—

----

[1] These sixteen lines are an amplification of some Gaelic lines quoted in
DR. GORDON'S *Iona*, p. 10 :—

> *Seachd bliadna roimh'n bhrath*
> *Thig muir thar* EIRIN *re aon trath*
> *'S thar* ILE *ghuirm ghlais*
> *Ach snamhaidh* I CHOLUIM *cleirich :*

which he renders : 'Seven years before the end of the world, a deluge shall
drown the nations : the sea, at one tide, shall cover Ireland and the green-
headed *Ilay*; but *Columba's* isle shall swim above the flood.'   He refers
previously to the opinion of some that this old prediction was one of the
reasons why so many monarchs chose the Island for their last resting-
place.

Then, as on rolling billows
  When the tornadoes die,
Rocks the great Solan calmly
  Where buried navies lie :
So riding, as God's token,
  Over the waters dark,
Our Columb's own Iona
  Shall be God's second Ark.

XXXV

Where'er our steps may wander
  In far-off ways of toil,
In longing sweet remembrance
  We tread thy sacred soil :
And when the toil is over
  Fain would we fall on sleep,
Where o'er thy first great Abbot
  Thine ocean breezes sweep ;
So when the Angel-trumpet
  Heralds the Easter-tide,
We may behold, as the mighty sound
Wakens the blessed sleepers round,
  Saint Columb at our side !

MISCELLANEOUS POEMS

Koimeterion:[1] An Ode

To a First Snowdrop in Mid-January

I

WHITE-ROBED little maiden,
Fair one, first to bring
Out of winter's Aidenn [2]
Earnest of the Spring :

II

Brown the beds about thee,
Chill and bare in death,
Sceptic East winds flout thee,
Scorn upon their breath !

III

But thy bell, it ringeth
Stilly on and on,
And thy silence singeth
' Koimeterion ';

[1] Koimeterion = Gk. κοιμητήριον = Eng. cemetery, or sleeping-place.
[2] The only authority known to the author for the adaptation of Aidenn from the Greek ἀίδης or ἀΐδης is that of Edgar A. Poe in *The Raven*.

IV

'Here they are but sleeping,
    Dreaming of the morn,
Souls, a vigil keeping,
    Waiting to be born :

V

'Souls of leaves and grasses,
    Souls of flower and fruit,
Here, till winter passes,
    Fast asleep in root.'

VI

Tell thy sweet evangel,
    Lovely little one !
Boldly like an angel,
    Softly like a nun :

VII

Angel-like in station
    By the doors of doom,
With thy revelation
    Rolling back the gloom.

VIII

Or, with saintly splendour,
  Lone in spirit-night,
Exquisitely tender,
  Tremulously bright,

IX

Like St. Agnes stealing
  Down the turret stair :
One small lamp revealing
  Love and life are there.

X

Life of blithe transition—
  Garden out of grave—
Loving manumission
  For each winter slave.

XI

But what means thy drooping ?
  Prone thy virgin bloom !
Like a statue stooping
  Silent o'er the tomb.

XII

‘Vigil is not sorrow !
　Hopefully look *down*,
There is the to-morrow,
　Thence the vernal crown.

XIII

‘Patience is not sadness !
　That is one with *this* :
Hope of coming gladness
　Is a present bliss.

XIV

‘Look ! they stir in slumber,
　Moving ere they spring
Flower-lives out of number,
　Past imagining !

XV

‘Then the full awaking !
　Drowsy night is past ;
Beauteous outbreaking !
　Full and free and fast.

XVI

'And, oh list ! fruition
　Is in sound as light :
Music marries vision :
　Singing kisses sight !

XVII

'Woodland loves long waiting
　Find their life anew :
All the birds a-mating
　Carol as they woo.

XVIII

'Soft airs, fleeting showers,
　Tender sunny gleams,
Court the budding bowers,
　Kiss the merry streams.

XIX

'And all fair things follow :
　Comes the cuckoo soon :
Comes the summer swallow :
　Comes the harvest moon :
O

XX

'Comes the autumn-glory :
Comes the winter rest ;
All tides tell their story—
Which is not the best?'

XXI

White-robed little maiden,
Look will I and list!
Of the under-Aidenn
Prime evangelist.

Ishmael's Song

I

My God hath heard me : I am His :
    The Lord my God is mine :
And mine are His—in Ishmael
    Is bless'd all Ishmael's line :
For of my seed for multitude
    Be yonder stars the sign.

II

Man's foe for ever—there shall reign
    No King for me but God !
Mine is this wild, and mine shall be,
    Sand-tract, oasis-sod :
Beneath no sceptre shall I kneel
    Except beneath His rod.

III

He will ride with me as I ride
    Great Paran's wastes along,

And give His angel-winds a charge
  To sing His Archer's song [1]
Of Ishmael evermore the free
  And evermore the strong !

IV

All ends of earth, times of all time,
  As here the blessed well,
As Lahairoi,[2] in light and life,
  My right divine shall tell,
For He the LORD my GOD is true
  And I am Ishmael ! [3]

[1] Gen. xxi. 20.

[2] Beer-lahai-roi, that is, 'the well of him that liveth and seeth me.'— (Gen. xvi. 14.)

[3] Ishmael, that is, 'God shall hear.'

A Night Storm on the Shropshire Hills

A SEPTEMBER DREAM

I HEAR the sea roar in the land of dreams.
  No wonted murmur of the water world
  Beneath the moon—but, all ' confusedly hurled,'
Its billows like Niagara's torrent-streams
War with each other, while the shingle screams
  'Neath hollow cliffs, and the Deep calls the Deep—
  The Air the Ocean,—with the whirlwind sweep,
And thunders crashing close on levin gleams.
I wake : and lo, the storm is of the land !
  The rush of mountain blast, the shrieking trees,
  The chimney roar—these are my visioned seas,
Not less sufficing, not less fiercely grand.
  O wild wind-onset on this mountain shore !
  Night for enchanted memory evermore.

The Maiden at the Well

I

AT the Well's heart serene and deep
Sweet waters lie:
But from their sleep
The maid will stir them by and by.

II

The plunging pail their peace shall break:
And at the sound
They shall awake,
Meeting the summons with a bound:

III

Then from the darkness to the light
Shall be new-born;
While in their sight
Is spread the beauty of the morn.

IV

Was their repose a blessèd thing?
For bliss or bane
Shall they up-spring?
Is such emotion joy or pain?

V

Deep in the maiden's heart serene
　　Sweet waters lie,
　　Silent, unseen—
But *one* shall stir them by and by !

VI

Love, that has lain in sleepy night,
　　Aroused shall sing
　　And leap to light,
As from still Winter leaps the Spring.

VII

But was the slumber good or ill ?
　　Will joy or pain
　　The future fill ?
Is such new knowledge true or vain ?

VIII

True be the knowledge that shall crown
　　Her waiting eyes !
　　Cast her not down,
Saying, ' "Tis folly to be wise !'

Where the Shade is

'He stands brightly where the shade is,
With the keys of Death and Hades.'
     MRS. BARRETT BROWNING'S *Fourfold Aspect.*

I

WHERE the shade is stands the LORD—
    When the sun of youth has set,
        When each spell is fading fast,
        And the dreamer wakes at last,
    And surprise and pain have met—
Where the shade is stands the LORD.

II

Where the shade is stands the LORD—
    When again and yet again
        Phantom forms of fear or ill
        Crowd against the tottering will,
    And the struggle seems in vain—
Where the shade is stands the LORD.

III

Where the shade is stands the LORD—
    When within the broken home
        All life's bread seems turned to stone :
        Death has come to one alone,

To the other will not come—
Where the shade is stands the LORD.

IV

Where the shade is stands the LORD—
    When the faint or fighting breath,
        When the drooped or glazing eye,
        Shows the gates of gloom are nigh,
    Opening to the Vale of Death—
Where that shade is stands the LORD.

V

Where the shade was stood the LORD—
    Then life's light won by Life's loss—
        Light that burned the dark away,
        Soft and sweet and strong as day—
    Streamed from His all-conquering Cross—
Where the shade was stood the LORD.

VI

Where *our* shade is, stand, O LORD!
    Make us see Thee in our night,
        Hear Thy promise through the gloom:
        'Lo, I have the keys of doom,
    O My children of the light!
Where your shade is stands your LORD.'

A Morning by the Sea

ON HAYLING ISLAND

(From Good Words)

'Twas Hayling Island and a summer day :
One out of few, although the month was June ;
But this one lay a calm between the storms,
And prized the more : so wild a memory
Of that which had been, and so great a fear
Of that which surely follow'd—roaring winds
And ceaseless rain—possessed us, that we said,
'This is the crown of summer,' and rejoiced,
Alien so long from light and liberty,
As only prisoners can, set free for once
From dismal durance.

           Down the shore we ranged,
Five elders and of children three times three.
The elders, wives and husbands, two and two,
And I, a solitary, come, they said,
To look and learn in view of wedded bliss—

To look and learn and mend my lonely ways.
The children, lads and lasses fresh and fair—
One they called 'May,' but sweeter than that May
The poets sing ; and, ever up and down,
A 'Will o' the Wisp'; and one 'Sir Percy' hight,
And one yclept 'the Duchess,' stately maid
Three summers old ; and others nameless here—
Were four and four, and eke a nondescript,
A slumb'rous thing, long-robed, expressionless,
Without the power of language, yet withal
A mine of vocal possibilities,
Whereon I gazed in fear lest cruel chance
Should rouse this Etna in its mother's arms
To burst in wrath upon the day's repose,
With cries imperious.
              Last, but not the least
(O larger thou than any nondescript !),
A curly-coated champion of the boys,
Who, plunging ever in the plunging wave,
Or chasing conies down the sandy ridge,
Did all their pleasure with a ready will,
One Sancho Panza—such his name—esquire
To four Don Quixotes. Yet is he himself
Worthy of knighthood. Thou of simple soul,

High courage, loyal will, and loving heart!
O good at need, when need is of the strong,
The true, the patient!   Paragon of dogs,
Lo, here I knight thee with my grey goose quill!
Wont ever at a bidding to 'lie down,'
Take this poetic pat on thy broad brows
And rise 'Sir Sancho'!   Immortality
(It is the poet's guerdon, little else
Has he, forsooth, to give) henceforth be thine!
And yet, O single-minded, as I look
And jest of fame to thee, thine eyes declare
'Fame's but a foolish guerdon, master mine!'
Careless art thou of all the blatant world,
And wiser than thy master, whom alone
Thou watchest with those trustful anxious eyes
For all the meed of praise that thy great heart
Holds ever precious.   Let him learn of thee,
He has his Master.

           Down the shore we ranged,
And drank the rushing river of the air,
Fresh, fragrant, sunny-clear; and with the expanse
Of the two oceans of the seas and heavens
Fed heart and mind.   Profound as Love the one,
A tideless depth of blue—with floating clouds,

The changeful Polynesia of the skies—
Tender in tone as it is fathomless
To vision ; and the other bright as Life,
When youth is strong and pure and beautiful,
And makes its own all lights of love and hope
That sparkle o'er it, and to every breath,
That blows a brave blast or inspires a dream,
Bounds in the joyous confidence of strength
And consciousness of beauty.
                      Tired at last,
Among the sand-hills sloping from the shore,
We lay at length and watch'd the sea and sky,
And, far away, the lovely garden-isle,
And, near at hand, the lowly fort that frown'd
And sentinelled the bay.   More still the breeze
And fuller was the sunshine, and our tongues
Grew stiller also, and our hearts more full
With sense of peace : heaven seemed to join the
      world,
So pure the peace.
                  Peace? Heaven was far away,
And this was earth ; or there was war in heaven !
Peace !—as we mused and dreamed, on our repose
Broke such a thunder !   O'er the fort a cloud

White, ghastly, rising scared our alien eyes,
Then—ere our minds were sentient—a roar
Shook earth and air.   We started as men start
To meet a peril ; and the sleeping child
Awoke and wailed ; and o'er our heads a lark,
That had been making music all that hour,
Ceased singing ; and the hound sped to the hills
Baying, to find some quarry of his dreams
Dead in the hollows.   So that mighty Gun
Did 'murder sleep.'   But dreader than its roar
The shudder of the agonising air,
Wherethrough the great shot tore its pitiless way.
A shriek, a groan, a tremor as of a soul
In torture—so the live reluctant air
Made known its passion, as the death-bolt sped
And five times smote the seas that, stricken, raved
And hurled in angry witness up to heaven
A hundred feet of foam, or ere at last
It plunged to sullen rest four miles away.

　　Awe-struck we look'd and listen'd ; and again,
And yet again ; then, with the wonted end
Of things familiar, awe to wonder shrunk,
And wonder to a careless interest
That watch'd the target and ere long grew tired.

Then home we went by the familiar sea
That never tires; but ere we left the shore,
Between the foamy limit of the tide
And the deep golden splendour and dark green
Of the thick gorse behind, again we sat
And the boys sang—while the sea-organ rolled—
A song I made for them a year ago.

The Reason why Florence was called 'The Duchess'

DEDICATED TO F. C. B. AND K. L. B.

(From *Good Words*)

'NOT her name, but Florence,' such is
Katie's comment on 'the Duchess,'
When she hears your grace's title
Given you in due requital
Of an aspect most serenely
Soft and placid, yet so queenly,
From your little three-years' stature,
That one cannot doubt that nature
Has decreed by certain touches
To design *at least* a Duchess!

'When and why?' does Katie ask me,
Quite resolved to take to task me,

And to make me give a reason
For this nominal high treason,
Ere she will acknowledge duly
That you are 'the Duchess' truly!

Listen, Katie, listen other,
Each and every, sister, brother,
While I tell you all the history,
This aristocratic mystery!

On a day you should remember
In a holiday December,
While the gale without blew madly,
And the hearth-side firelight gladly
Smiled to scorn the winter wailing,
While we sat around it stilly—
Elders all but May and Willie—
On a sudden in came sailing
(Like a white swan on the waters
With two dingy cygnet daughters,
Or like queen through fabled gateway
Closed in fear behind her straightway,
'Twixt two griffins, by some charming
Kept in durance from all harming),

P

You, my Florence—a white figure,
'Twixt two cats, and not much bigger
Than the beasties you were bearing
With a baby's easy daring.
Little fingers could not hold them,
So the whole arm must enfold them
(Arms and fingers *minus* mittens),
These two taloned tabby kittens !
Big as cats, of savage feature,
Each a grim and gruesome creature.
Had *I* touched them, they 'd have scratched me,
Or, in will at least, despatched me ;
Or, if fearful more than frightening,
Have despatched themselves like lightning
From *my* arms' unlovely prison,
Mewing wild, ' I isn't his'n ! '

But, your Grace ! by all the Graces !
There they hung with charmèd faces,
From your wee white arms depending,
Heads and tails together blending,
Troubled, doubtless, if not tortured,
But, as apples hang in orchard,

There they hung, nor scratched nor bit you,
Spit nor swore, nor hurt a whit you !

Scratched *you*, bit *you*?   Just as soon a
Lion would have bitten Una !
Spit or swore at *you*?   Much rather
They 'd have spit at Tim their father,
Or have sworn at Tib their mother,
Or have eaten one another,
Like the cats who at Kilkenny
Found each other one too many !

Ah, my darling ! at this vision,
'Spite the prosy world's derision,
I confess, so did it win me,
The poor poet spirit in me
Rose and spread its folded pinion,
With a moment's sweet dominion
In the regions sunny, airy,
Of far Eld and farther Faery,
And in you there passed before me—
Such a charm and spell was o'er me—
Those who formed the darling fancies
Of our childhood's blithe romances.

Said I so?   Not I!   I tumbled
Back to earth and merely mumbled,
' Look, her grace and glamour such is,
'Tis no baby, but a duchess !'

There, my pet, you have the reason
For this nominal high treason !

ﬀour ﬂoets: A ﬂersonal ﬁistory

(1877)

I

WALTER SCOTT

MASTER-MAGICIAN of that breezy Spring
  Ere my first decade died—when life awoke
  Within me of the mystic world, and broke
In such illuming flashes as still fling
Light on my soul—in bugle-calls that ring
  Still in mine ears! thy wand it was whose stroke
  As swift in power as April's on the oak,
Stirred all my life to rich imagining.
O glamour not of love or ladies' eyes,
  But of the stream, the mountain, and the glen,
  Of war-horse champing, clash of armoured men,
And song that, like its subject, never dies!
  Master-Romancer, not supreme to-day,
  Power yet was thine which cannot pass away.

II

ELIZABETH BARRETT BROWNING

THEN with the early summer came the zest
    For food not meet for babes—for old-world lore
    Ere ' Pan was dead ' [1]—for fervent thought to soar
Where sang ' The Seraphim ' [2]—or, in anxious quest,
To plunge through deep seas at the soul's behest,
    And find with beating heart and bated breath
    How knowledge is by suffering, life by death [3]—
White Pearls of truth 'neath Ocean's darkling breast.
AURORA,[4] from thine hand the summer long
    I drank the ' Wine of Cyprus ': [5] with thine eyes
    I saw from ' out the depths ' [6] to the clear skies,
And heard thy voice sing true the spheric song.[7]
    More than our ' England's Sappho ' [8] is thy due :
    Earth's Sovereign Poetess, as great as true.

[1] *The Dead Pan*, vol. iii., 4th Edition, 1856.
[2] *Ibid.*, vol. i.
[3] See *Vision of Poets, Ibid.*, vol. i.
[4] *Aurora Leigh*—the title of her most important work. It is in some sort autobiographical.
[5] See vol. iii., 4th Edition, 1856.
[6] See ' De Profundis ' in *Last Poems*, 1862.
[7] See Sonnet, *Perplexed Music*, vol. ii., 4th Edition, 1856.
[8] A title given to the poetess by Edgar A. Poe.

ALFRED TENNYSON

Ere this, and in the fuller year, there fell
  On mind and soul made ready long ago—
  Receptive ground for such an overflow,
Nile-like, of grace from mystic hills—a spell
Of power made sweet by music's miracle,
  That showed stern truth, high duty, steeped i'
    the glow
  Of such fair trust my restless heart below
Answered far Heaven at last with ' All is well.'[1]
I swear, O Poet, by thy ' Voices '[2] twain,
  By souls that cannot prove and yet believe,[3]
  By Love and Duty, by Saint Agnes' Eve,
By Arthur, Galahad, Gareth, and their train,
  Thou art the Master-Prophet of this age :
  Its sweetest music-maker, surest sage.

[1] See Section cxxvi. in *In Memoriam.*
[2] *The Two Voices.*
[3] See Proemion to *In Memoriam.*

JOHN KEBLE

'THE richest glow sets round th' autumnal sun':[1]
    And so about the later year there grew
    A light of holier influence, deeper hue,
Than that which fell so fresh on life begun,
Or that the radiant summer ever won,
    A light which brought, with all things fair and new,
    That spiritual City clear in view
Where the true life begins 'when life is done.'[2]
Priest-Poet,—Phosphor of the LIGHT OF LIGHT,
    'SUN of my soul'—still is the singing sweet
    Of those high Poets, beautiful their feet
Still on the hills which darken toward the night,
    But thy deep voice is tenderest in mine ear,
    Nearest thy saintly presence and most dear.

[1] See *Christian Year*, 2nd Sunday after Epiphany.
[2] *Ibid.*

EAST-END VERSES, ETC.

From Windermere

MOORED by a green isle of Winandermere—
    Listening the gentlest lapping of the wave
    On the rock margin, and the blackbirds' brave
Soldierly antiphons, afar and near,
And the wind's whispered evensong—I hear
    A sound beyond, and sweeter as more grave
    Than ever paradise of nature gave,
Dear to my heart of old, and now more dear:
The roar of London—the deep undersong,
    The myriad music of immortal souls
High-couraged, much-enduring, midst the long
    Drear toil and gloom and weariness.   It rolls
Over me with all power, for in its tone
The hearts I love in CHRIST beat with my own.

'𝕿𝖍𝖊 𝕲𝖆𝖗𝖉𝖊𝖓 𝖔𝖋 𝖙𝖍𝖊 𝕷𝖔𝖗𝖉'

'The desert shall rejoice and blossom as the rose.'—(ISAIAH xxxv. 1.) (*Motto of All Saints', Mission Church of St. Paul's, Haggerston.*)

'The Lord shall comfort Zion: He will comfort all her waste places: and He will make her wilderness like Eden, and her desert like the Garden of the Lord. Joy and gladness shall be found therein, thanksgiving, and the voice of melody.'—(ISAIAH li. 3.)

THE GARDEN that has been, and is no more!
　　And left the world forlorn of bliss and bloom;
　　Nought but the flaming sword to break the gloom,
Guarding against all hope the fatal Door.
The GARDEN now! peaceful amid the roar
　　Of circling storm—CHRIST'S Church, in face of
　　　doom
　　Revealing pardon—by the desolate tomb
Spreading the fruits of life in plenteous store.
The GARDEN that shall be! where none shall know
　　Of noise, or gloom, or grave, or curse again;
　　But, 'neath th' unsetting Sun and gracious Rain,
The Rose and Lily evermore shall blow.
　　GARDENER of souls! dear LORD, we work for Thee,
　　Sure of this beauteous Eden that shall be.

𝔄 𝔖on of t𝔥e 𝔐ission

JOHN SHELDRICK

Died Sept. 7th, 1894.   Aged 50

He was confirmed at St. Paul's, and received his first Communion at the Mission Church, and his last on his deathbed, August 30th, 1894.

'The desert shall rejoice and blossom as the rose.'—(*Motto of the Mission.*)

'SON of our Mission : rough-hewn were thy ways,
  Till on thy life the Church of JESUS smiled :
And reared thee to thy peace and to His praise
  A rose within the wild.'

' Hire for all the Day '

ONE spake—I know not who—a word of power :
　　He saw his child in cruel suffering lie,
And through each sad day, and at that dread hour
　　Wherein he watched his martyr moan and die,
　　While others asked their spirit-stricken ' Why ? '
Earth's doubt divinely did he put away ;
　　And looking with strong faith's far-visioned eye,
He to his heart and theirs did simply say,
' *One hour of toil : full hire for all the day.*'

Great-hearted Christian ! true philosopher :
　　Beholding things that are by things to be :
No natural tears thine heaven-lit eyes could blur,
　　Flow as they would, and did, all piteously—
　　Eyes of high trust from all soul-dimness free,
As gold of the Refiner hath no dross—
　　They saw Ascension's crowned eternity
Beyond the seeming-cruel Glade and Cross :
Beyond life's bitterest pain, and final loss.

An East-End Schoolmaster

ALFRED UNITT

(In Memoriam)

TRUE, strong, and noble !   O my son, my friend,
  Type of the steadfast English force and will,
  Ever in sternness tender-hearted still ;
The vigorous man, th' unconscious child, did blend
In thee so purely, neither had its end
  Unmixed, alone—Love's light was on the Hill ;
  The Plain was fed by that sweet-flowing rill
O'er which winds whisper and the wild flowers bend.
GOD give us, in our grief, to be like thee !
  Strong to endure, yet child-like 'neath His Hand—
The Hand that—in a life more full, more free,
  Where no death-cloud may darken o'er the land—
Has led thee on, past all these cares and woes,
To some diviner service and repose.

Together

(In Memoriam)

WILLIAM HENRY JARVIS, aged 8   ⎫ Who fell ⎧ Aug. 31st, 1890.
ALFRED JAMES NORGROVE, aged 13 ⎬ asleep in ⎨ Sept. 3rd, 1890.
ALICE MAUD HALL, aged 20   ⎭ CHRIST ⎩ Sept. 11th, 1890.

'Called, and chosen, and faithful.'—(REV. xiv. 15.)

So young, yet 'called'; so short your pilgrim way,
     Yet ye were 'chosen' as the proved and strong;
     Not filling the twelve hours of labour long,
Yet counted 'faithful' as the worn and grey;
Your service light, your 'hire for all the day'!
     Oh, to lament would do your guerdon wrong!
     You who have passed into the light and song,
Far from earth's discord and life's sad decay.
Now, loving Willie, your dear master[1] greet,
     So early lost, so quickly found again!
Sing, happy choir-boy,[2] at your Saviour's feet,
     Where soars in Paradise a nobler strain.
And hearken, gentle daughter, in your rest,
With ears unstopped,[3] the converse of the blest.

[1] While W. H. J. was lying ill, the young Headmaster of his school (Mr. A. Unitt), to whom he was much attached, lay dying (see preceding Sonnet).

[2] A. J. N. was one of the Senior Choir Boys of St. Paul's, Haggerston.

[3] A. M. H. had suffered for years from incurable deafness.

ﬀreﬞderick Arnold[1]

(From *The Guardian*, October 28th, 1891)

'DEAR ARNOLD, life is less by loss of thee :
  Less full, less jocund.   Hours with thee sped by
  On wings of wit, or wealth of sympathy,
Or talk on truths of height and depth, yet free
Ever from cant or affectation.   We,
  In our stern East-End life, grew bright of eye
  And cheerier at thy comings !   Smile or sigh
Fitted thy various converse equally,
Sweet-hearted friend !   Alas, that now no more
  The arm-chair or the pulpit will be filled
  With that kind presence—keen attention thrilled
By tales of 'men and cities,' or the lore
Of those book-depths from which thou knew'st so well
To mix for mind or heart an œnomel.'[2]

---

[1] This Sonnet is placed among those of the East-End selection because of Mr. Arnold's many visits to its clergy and his genial help during a period of twenty-one years.

[2] *Antholog. Palat*, 12, 165.

F. M. A.

(In Memoriam)

GOD-DAUGHTER, now with GOD : with us, for thee,
    Though rapt so soon, no pang at heart may dwell :
We hear a song of thine beyond the sea
    That drowns thy funeral bell.

A Fighter

I

'I was ever a fighter—so one fight more ':
    Sang the Bard ere his death ;
The spirit of man till the earth-time is o'er
    Must be bold fighter's breath.

II

Wherever he chance on the forces of sin
    (And where chance will he not ?)
'Gainst the legions without, or the giants within,
    Cast each Crusader's lot !

III

Without are the cruelty, vice, and despair
    Of the wild world astray :
The enemy's presence that sickens the air
    Down our Monarch's highway.

IV

Within are the sophistries, subtleties, lies :
  The false guides of the blind :
Devil-lures for the flesh in a fair disguise :
  The doubt-ghosts of the mind.

V

On, Fighter ! on, Churchman ! on, Patriot, on !
  Marching orders for you :
'Wherever sin-sadness is under the sun
  There is fighting to do.'

Holiday Ode to the North-West Wind

BY AN EAST-ENDER

I

Blow, breeze, from the north and the west,
   Through the clear afternoon ;
To all that gives solitude zest,
To the zeal, not the languor, of rest
   Our tired spirits attune.

II

Blow, breeze, in the deep of the night,
   Solemn-sweet in our ears,
God's organ of full-toned delight,
With thine ebbings and flowings of might,
   Charm our souls from their fears.

III

Blow again, potent breeze, with the morn,
   Till, refreshed with thy wine,
Eyes dim, spirits harassed and worn
Looking now on past pains with sweet scorn,
   May arise and may shine !

ELEGIAC POEMS

Lord of Death

I

In the cold caverns of the deep of night
   Cleaves the still air a kingly clarion's breath,
With voice as vivid as a meteor light:
   'Our LORD is Lord of Death.'

II

Then lay His dead to rest high-heartedly
   And purely, 'neath green grasses or blue waves:
Faith, Hope, and Love their sentinels hard by
   On guard above their graves.

Before Gordon's Monument

'Have we forgotten Gordon?'—(TENNYSON)

I

Look on this man who never feared a man
    Or multitude of men, whose regal life
    Was such a calm amid perpetual strife,
That inly like an Eden stream it ran :
Because he feared God, and because that fear
Was a child's reverence for a Father dear.

II

An Eden stream : its source behind the bars
    Of that strong gate kept by the flaming brand,
    Within the limits of the lovely land
Where God walks in the noon, and 'neath the stars,
And all about Him moves a mystic throng
In light and strength, and in repose and song.

III

An Eden stream which mossy margins laved,
    Or fed the fairest flowers that ever grew,
    Of all sweet fragrance and of every hue ;
While, underneath, the lithe weed-tresses waved

Long coils of grace, and in its coves of calm
The great pure lilies floated, breathing balm.

IV

A stream that met the cheerful kiss of morn ;
   Flashed back, responsive, all the smiles of noon ;
   That dreamed its mystic dream beneath the moon,
And knew the charm on the last breezes borne,
And mixed its murmurs down the darksome vale
With the lone music of the nightingale.

V

This was his soul : a soul that flowed apart
   From common sight—far off from eye and ear
   Of common men ; so deep, so pure, so clear,
So sentient of the beating of GOD's heart
In this the world once made so good—a soul
That from the little could conceive the whole,

VI

'GOD's will'; and seeing, could be satisfied,
   And flow serenely.   Sure that all was well,
   From the world's matin-chime to evening bell,
In all that breathed and grew, or failed and died :
And, so, receptive of all signs of love,
Here in the depth, there in the height above.

VII

A soul that knew not self: that loved the sky,
   But not earth less, and all things intervene:
   Because he loved that Heart and Hand unseen
That planned, and framed, and unto all were nigh,
And which he knew were Love; and in the range
Of wildest circumstance could never change.

VIII

But out of Eden all the wide world through
   That strong stream ran; no limit barred its course.
   Through frost and fire, through light or dark, its
      force
Sped, gathering volume, until all men knew—
All that could hear and see—that once again
A Warrior-Prophet had been given to men.

IX

A Warrior: the strong hand, the set square chin,
   The high, broad helm of brow, the forward gaze
   That spake unconsciously the scorn of praise,
Spiritual light telling of fire within;
Withal, the simple manner, plain and mild—
This Warrior-Prophet, who was yet a child,

X

How did he shake the time, and shame the crew
   Of lounging idlers and self-serving slaves!
   And, where the Banner of the Cross still waves
For spirits pure and high—the knightly few—
How did he hearten hope, spur and inspire,
Kindling new purpose at his own soul's fire!

XI

A Prophet-Warrior.   Though his words were deeds
   They preached GOD's truth, from England to
      Cathay,
   And last in Egypt—whence he went his way—
Against our selfish aims, our gauds, our greeds,
Our vulgar pleasures, and our vulgar fears,
Our empty glorying, or our cynic sneers.

XII

And, 'last in Egypt'—where he was not found
   Because GOD took him.   Warrior's work was done,
   Prophet's word spoken.   And yet both go on—
Nothing of GOD can pass, of sight or sound!
Flashes the sword still of CHRIST's knight!   His word
Still, like a trumpet, in the land is heard.

XIII

O waste Soudan, through him thou art not waste !
   Never in all the ages can be hid
   Thy claim to have him for thy pyramid !
Thine, for thou hold'st him !   We, in all our haste
Of word or work, see how amidst thy sands
His ghostly figure, like a Pharos, stands.

XIV

' Have we forgotten Gordon ? ' asks the seer—
   Best voice of England, ay, of Christendom ;—
   ' Have we forgotten Gordon ? '   Well, if some
(He knows who asks) no longer see and hear,
Now let this question, with its living breath,
Stir the dry bones within the vale of death.

XV

O Gordon, England's honour, yet her shame !
   Her *honour*—thou didst love as well as serve,
   And myriad loyal souls in heart and nerve
Beat quicklier, thrill noblier, at thy name—
And yet her *shame* : since shorn of chivalry
Her statecraft left thee in the waste, to die.

XVI

Martyr! confessing, may we be forgiven?
  Thy love would straight absolve us, and thy smile
  (Sweet-hearted hero!) free from selfish guile,
Free from self-pity, may look down from Eden
And say, 'My noble England, do GOD's will!
Be of good cheer, thou art His soldier still.'

XVII

I think that it is best—so, of GOD's will,
  That in that desert of the lone Soudan
  Should lie the relics of that knightly man;
Where, none can tell, nor can be told until
All things of heaven and earth, the far and nigh,
Shall have, one morning, their Epiphany.

XVIII

Best: for his life was hid with CHRIST in GOD—
  Therefore more eloquent to the hearing ear—
  (O power of such a life!)   So he 's more near
Than if we had him under churchyard sod:
More near: imagination is more rife;
Which means more high thought, more uplifted life.

XIX

Dead, hidden Gordon!   Thou art 'live and seen.
   That spiritual stream, in Eden born,
   After long day flowed back by night to morn—
Its orb of course complete ;—with fuller green
On margin, flowers more fair, and sweeter song,
Its waters wind those mystic lands along.

The Mother of a Saint

I

SHE said, 'I am the Mother of a Saint,
  Not of an angel—angels seem too far ;
We love a flower we touch as well as see
  More than the furthest star.

II

' My saint was first washed white from taint of birth
  By Word, in wave of the Atoning Spring :
And then went home ere she of sinful life
  Knew any thought or thing.

III

' A saint also by heritage of love :
  By meed of many a sacrificial prayer
Offered to GOD ere yet she sweetened sight
  And breathed this earthly air.

IV

' My Father took my little flower away
  In all its vernal, softly-scented bloom,
That it of falling, fading earthly days
  Might never know the doom.

R

V

‘ No, no, He did not take it all from me ;
  My FATHER would not rob me of my own ;
Had I no other dear one left to love
    I could not be alone.

VI

‘ She is not far—my saint—in very sooth
  No distance parts the spiritually dear ;
With those who love as we, the far-away
    Is never less the near.

VII

‘ My memory keeps all that my baby was ;
  My faith has visions fair of that she is ;
My love, I dare to think, is sweet to her,
    Part of her life in bliss.

VIII

‘ Thinks she not of me ?   Prays she not for me ?
  Is she not almost always at my side ?
My husband’s love is here ; my saint’s is there ;
    So am I satisfied.

IX

'Was not the sacrifice my Father asked—
　This parting—for her good and so for mine?
FATHER, 'twas surely for my greater good
　She should be safely Thine.

X

' "My good."　O fathers, mothers of the saints,
　A saint's life, all more saintly, ours must be !
Draw me, my baby, with the cords of love
　Closer to Love and thee.

XI

'So can no bitter ill-content be mine ;
　Some consecrated tears, but no complaint ;
Elect to be, by Easter grace of GOD,
　The Mother of a Saint.'

Tennyson: In Memoriam

Four Sonnets

(From *The Church Times*)

I

'OUR Master taken from our head to-day.'
　　Henceforth to some life cannot be the same,
　　Less lofty and less lovely.　Poor and tame
Is that which loses the absorbing ray
Which drew or swept the common mists away :
　　Which glowed with love, or flashed like angry
　　　　flame,
　　Made good more dear, and dealt with sin and
　　　　shame
Like Arthur's keen Excalibur in fray.
And no Elisha !　Light and sound agree ;
　　The birds are mute, the skies are ashen grey ;
The wet wind sobs along the stricken lea.
　　What is the world without a Poet?　Say
At least to England here, and over sea,
　　O caput mortuum sine animâ !

II

O English Singer, loving England so
    That in thy loss thine England lies forlorn :
    Where now 'the hate of hate, the scorn of scorn,
The love of love'?   We falter as we go
Like children orphaned.   Or for joy or woe
    Is there a voice authentic?   Morn to morn
    Succeeds : but nowhere, nowhere is there born
A King to say 'I love, I rule, I know.'
He knew our England, loved, and ruled it well—
    (What ruler like a poet?)—Ah, that hand
Has dropped both sword and sceptre.   Funeral bell
    For the great prophet is for all his land ;
Till some Elisha be God's oracle,
    Like him to curse, to comfort, to command.

III

What good things meet in thee! the sweet, the strong,
    The stately and the tender : pæan, psalm,
    Surge-thunder, bottomless ocean-depths of calm :
Harp-music : clarion peals of battle-song :
Anguish that thrills and wails for shame or wrong :
    The small home-daisy, the sea-circled palm :

Flute-notes of Spring, and Summer's scented balm—
All equally to thy great Muse belong.
Like Spenser, Poet of the Poets, thine
  Is a lyre exquisite of such melody
As proves thee peer amid the most divine
  O' the sacred guild ; yet thou art more than he,
More strong, more stern—less water in thy wine—
  Yet as serene in thy tranquillity.

IV

Gone : and no Singer near th' imperial height
  On which thy prophet feet were beautiful ;
  And heart is deadly sick, and brain is dull,
And eyes, expectant, with a blur on sight
Peer vaguely, doubtfully, into the night.
  God, Whose compassions fail not, in this lull
  Of song, have pity ! put us 'neath the rule
Of some true Poet singing in Thy light !—
For him who sang of reverence—Reverence :
  Of life-long duty—Following shall not fail :
Of patriot passion—Empire's firm defence
  Shall seal his teaching, let who will assail.
Of Christ—O stainless, selfless Innocence,
  Write, that he sang, sought, found the Holy Grail !

ffather Damien

I

FULL is the world of contrasts, and 'tis well.
So is the mind's eye caught, and so the heart
Finds its pulse quickened.   So we bear our part
In scenes where thought, uncharmed, would never
dwell.
Here is a contrast wide as Heaven and Hell :
Here GOD in Nature, and the Devil's art
At worst in dire disease ; here the fell smart
Of typical sin 'mid beauty's miracle.
Here, too, a tortured body, foul to sight,
And a great soul exalted above men,
Beautiful in the test of saintliest light !
Here Pain and Peace beyond all common ken ;
Here from an Isle of Death sounds through the night
A Name of life and morning, Damien.

II

Blow, Breeze of such a morning, on the vale
   Where the dry bones of self-indulgence lie :
   And, trumpet-tongued, let such a prophet-cry
Wake the self-loving from their sleep, nor fail
To spur our athletes to o'erleap the pale
   Of common duties and lift far and high
   The standard of that love which least can die
When calmly bidding ghastliest death ' All hail.'
Brave Priest, true Martyr, Preacher of thy LORD
   By mightiest example !   May thy name,
May the devotion of thy soul that soared
   Beyond all point of wonted noble aim,
For all high purpose in our hearts be stored,
   That our true following may be thy true fame.

III

So, Damien, thence—where horror reigns a while—
   From thy sad cell amid the summer seas,
   Where living death taints the Elysian breeze,
And hideous forms a Paradise defile—
Shall a diviner grace and beauty smile
   Than ever Nature gave to cheer or please,

And crown it midst the Oceanides
A new Iona—a new Holy Isle.
O beauty of a great pure life !   O power
  Of Christ-like love that never counts the cost ;
That works not for repute or for the hour ;
  That for the unloved, the exiled, the storm-tossed,
Whom life's most woful waves would fain devour,
  If only it may save, wills to be lost !

IV

Lost : as men reckon loss whose aims are pent
  Within the limit of the paltry span
  Of brute life—as if time were one with man—
Who feel naught of the noble discontent
Of an immortal, to whom time is lent
  For endless issues, by the eternal plan,
  And to whose soul there seems no greater ban
Than not to know that he for these was sent.
Lost ?   Damien, oh, to lose with thee, and gain,
  Far in the one true Island of the blest,
In that Pacific where ' is no more pain,'
  Fruition of the end of that great quest
With CHRIST, for CHRIST, to which His own attain,
  To which they were elected—*then* to rest !

The Passing of the Archbishop

(From *The Guardian*, 14th October 1896)

' He died on the Sunday morning after his return from Ireland.
He had received the Holy Communion in Hawarden Church at
eight, and, at eleven o'clock Matins, he fell from his knees during
the saying of the Absolution.'

I

So late the saintly herald over seas
    Of all high courage and all sweet accord :
Now lowly, by the altar, on his knees
    He passes to his LORD.

II

He passes over seas again : but now
    Who followed, goes to find the Holy Grail :
Before that Presence of his LORD to bow
    Which is beyond the veil.

III

Where shall be laid his dust?   In yonder hold
    Where England lifts her stateliest towers on high ;
Hard by the altar of his peers of old
    Let the great Churchman lie.

William Hill

Ob. September 5th, 1885

' HE scorned delights and lived laborious days ';
  No common pleasures won his mind or will ;
  No joys of self so large a heart could fill,
Nor stooped he ever to the lust of praise.
Yet was his toil a joy to him always !
  And so, like some broad river strong and still,
  His life flowed sweetly, but with power, until
It found the ocean depth beyond our gaze.
Yet we who year by year beheld it flow
  Do trust that somewhat of its strength and calm
Has passed into our souls, and that we know
  How life may be a sermon and a Psalm.
O simple stately soul ! childlike and wise,
What genius shone serenely in thine eyes !

The Duchesse d'Alençon

(From *Church Bells*)

A young lady, who was assisting the Duchesse d'Alençon at her stall, says :—

'I grasped the Duchess by the waist and repeated, dragging her along, "Come, Madame! You must really come"; but she shook me off, saying, "No, no! I stay." Half-suffocated, and already attacked by the flames, I was forced to leave the Duchess, and she remained motionless scarcely two steps from her stall, her eyes raised to Heaven as if she beheld a vision.'

Mlle. d'Andlau, who was likewise close by the Duchess, and exclaimed to her, 'Let us escape!' says :—

'The Duchess, whose whole anxiety was to save the girls around her, calmly replied, "Go fast before us ; go out fast. Do not trouble about me ; I shall leave last." These were certainly the Princess's last words.'

See *Times'* 'Own Correspondent,' Paris, May 7th, 1897.

'*I shall leave last.*'   Calmly and nobly said :

Calmly, in saintly trust and courtly grace ;

Nobly, as best became her knightly race,

Her living Great and her immortal Dead.

So can sweet Peace and stately Courage wed.

Heaven shone more surely on that upward face,

Now that the last dread Foe drew on apace,

With all that hissing Hell about him spread.

Did ever earthly greatness farther go,
  While earthly life was at its last and worst?
We know the elect of both worlds, for we know
  Who said—Himself of all this world accurst—
' Here lose thyself; thine the last place below :
  Then come up higher, for My last is first.'

𝔖𝔞𝔫𝔠𝔥𝔬: 𝔄𝔫 𝔒𝔩𝔡 𝔉𝔯𝔦𝔢𝔫𝔡

A large brown Irish retriever: buried in the Vicarage Garden of St. Paul's, Haggerston: a stone to his memory is on the school wall, with this inscription :—

'In the centre of this lawn lies

SANCHO

a gentleman in all but humanity; thorough-bred, single in mind, true of heart; for seventeen years the faithful and affectionate friend of his master, who loved him, and now for him "faintly trusts the larger Hope" contained, it may be, in Romans viii. 19-21.

He died, April 26, 1883.'

NOT sparse of friends the world has been to me
　　By grace of GOD; sweetness and light to life
　　Their love has given; many a stormy strife,
Many a pulseless torpor, on my sea,
Through them—their presence or their memory—
　　Have been or stilled or quickened; and to thee
　　My Dog, the tribute, as the term, is due,
My *Friend!* not least of all dear, near, and true
These seventeen years—and through the years to be
　　Sure in my heart of immortality.
　　Must this be all?　I' the great Day of the LORD,
Shall aught that is of good and beauty now
　　Be missing?　Shall not each gift be restored?
　　Paul says 'the whole creation'—why not thou?

HYMNS

The Father

'I believe in God the Father Almighty, Maker of heaven and earth.'

I

NONE else but Thee for evermore,
One, All, we dread, believe, adore :
Great earth and heaven shall have their day
And, worn and old, shall pass away,
But Thou remainest on Thy throne,
Eternal, changeless, and alone !

II

None else we praise ! in every form,
In peace of calm, and power of storm,
In simple flower, and mystic star,
In all around, and all afar,
In grandeur, beauty, truth, but Thee
None else we hear, none else we see.

III

None else we love ! for sweeter grace
That made anew a ruined race :

The heirs of life, the lords of death,
With earliest voice and latest breath,
When days begin, when days are done,
Bless we the FATHER for the SON!

IV

None else we trust! though flesh may fail,
Or heart may sink when foes assail,
Thou, by Thy SPIRIT, art our stay,
And peace that shall not pass away:
None else in life and death have we,
But we have all in all with Thee!

V

Yea, none but Thee all worlds confess,
And those redeemed ones numberless:
FATHER, with SON and SPIRIT, One,
And evermore beside Thee none.
Of all that is, has been, shall be,
We praise, love, trust none else but Thee!

Amen.

The Son

'And in Jesus Christ, His only Son our Lord.'

I

God the Father's only Son,
And with Him in glory One,
One in wisdom, One in might,
Absolute and Infinite :
Jesu ! I believe in Thee,
Thou art Lord and God to me.

II

Preacher of eternal peace,
Christ, anointed to release,
Setting wide the dungeon door
Unto sinners chained before :
Jesu ! I believe in Thee,
Prophet sent from God to me.

III

Low in sad Gethsemane,
High on dreadful Calvary,
In the garden, on the Cross,
Making good our utter loss :

Jesu! I believe in Thee,
Priest and Sacrifice for me.

IV

Ruler of Thy ransomed race,
And Protector by Thy grace,
Leader in the way we wend,
And Rewarder at the end:
Jesu! I believe in Thee,
Christ, the King of kings to me.

V

Light revealed through clouds of pain,
That the blind might see again;
Love, content in death to lie,
That the dead might never die:
Jesu! I believe in Thee,
Light, and Love, and Life to me.

VI

All my longing heart would know
While I watch and wait below;
All that I would find above,
All of everlasting love:
Jesu! I believe in Thee,
Thou art All in all to me.   Amen.

The Holy Ghost

I

God the Spirit, we adore Thee,
   In the trinal Godhead One,
One in love, and power, and glory,
   With the Father and the Son;
Prayer and praise to Thee we bring,
Our devotion's offering.

II

Once the desolate world-ocean,
   Quickened from its long death-sleep,
Woke to light and life's emotion,
   At Thy brooding o'er its deep;
Spirit, ever may Thy breath
Quicken us from sleep and death.

III

Holy fount of inspiration,
   By Whose gift the great of old
Spake the word of revelation,
   Marvellous and manifold,

Grant to us who see and hear
Reverence of eye and ear.

IV

Priceless Gift of CHRIST for ever,
　　Righteousness and peace and joy,
Which the evil world, that never
　　Can receive, cannot destroy,
Shall the Church or faint or fear
While the Comforter is near?

V

Author of our new creation,
　　Giver of the second birth,
May Thy ceaseless renovation
　　Cleanse our souls from stains of earth
And our bodies ever be
Holy temples meet for Thee.

VI

When we wander, LORD, direct us,
　　Keep us in the Master's way,
Let Thy strong, swift sword protect us,
　　Warring in the evil day;

PARACLETE for every need,
Come to strengthen and to lead !

VII

Come, Thy glorious gifts providing,
    Foretaste of the future, now,
Bring that sweet sense of abiding
    Thou canst give, and only Thou :
One in Thee, we shall be one,
In the FATHER and the SON.   Amen.

The Incarnation

' He was conceived by the Holy Ghost, born of the Virgin Mary.'

I

THE SON forsook the FATHER'S home
For mercy to lost man,
And did not scorn the Virgin's womb
To bear the sinner's ban.

II

Meekly the Maiden pure believed
The great Archangel's word,
And by the HOLY GHOST conceived
The Saviour, CHRIST the LORD.

III

The word made flesh creation sees :
Its mighty GOD in man :
The mystery of mysteries
Since time on earth began !

IV

That we might gain a second birth
The Holy SON was given :
'Twas GOD Himself came down to earth
To win us back to heaven.

V

Lord ! we believe with love and praise
    This wondrous truth of Thee :
Thereby in all our troublous days
    How strong henceforth are we !

VI

So near art Thou, so strong are we,
    For now, if we are Thine,
Our Brother in humanity,
    Thou makest us divine !

VII

We see with peace in times of fear
    Thy human Face and Form ;
Thy human Voice with joy we hear
    Sweet-toned above the storm.

VIII

So dread we not the deathly strife
    Knowing that Thou hast died,
It can but bear us into life,
    Since nearer to Thy side ! Amen.

The Atonement

' He suffered under Pontius Pilate, was crucified, dead, and buried.'

I

My Saviour! I behold Thy life
 Of scarce one smile and many tears ;
I mark the spiritual strife,
 Thy human woes, Thy human fears,
And cry, ' Was ever grief like Thine,
Or debt of sin so vast as mine ? '

II

I watch thine agonising hour,
 I see Thee by Thine own betrayed,
Alone in Pilate's craven power,
 And scourged and scornfully arrayed,
And cry, ' Was ever grief like Thine,
Or debt of sin so vast as mine ? '

III

I see Thee fainting on Thy way,
   Reviled and mocked of all the throng,
I hear the bitter words they say,
   The abject's curse, the drunkard's song,
And cry, ' Was ever grief like Thine,
Or debt of sin so vast as mine ? '

IV

That sin in every taunt I hear,
   And see in every look of scorn ;
It is the Cross which Thou dost bear,
   The sharpness of Thy crown of thorn ;
Dear LORD, ' Was ever grief like Thine,
Or debt of sin so vast as mine ? '

V

My Saviour, I behold Thy death,
   I hear Thy cries, Thy last words seven,
I see the scowling gaze beneath,
   Above, the darkened face of Heaven,
And cry, ' Was ever grief like Thine,
Or debt of sin so vast as mine ? '

VI

My Saviour, I behold Thy grave
   In that still garden's awful gloom,
I see Thee lying there to save
   My soul from an eternal tomb,
And cry, 'Was ever grief like Thine,
Or debt of sin so vast as mine?'

VII

And yet with all I hear and see
   Of Death, or Passion of Thy life,
Sweet hopes are ministered to me
   And voices fall with comfort rife,
That say, 'Because He lived and died,
From sin thou canst be purified!'   Amen.

The Resurrection of the Lord

' He descended into hell ; the third day He rose again
from the dead.'

I

ALL the sacrifice is ended,
  Breathed His Body's latest breath,
And His human Soul hath wended
  Where the weary rest beneath ;
CHRIST as Man hath comprehended
  All the human law of death.

II

Yet not there His Soul remaineth
  Nor His body in the tomb :
Lo ! what sudden glory gaineth
  Quick dominion o'er the gloom !
Lo ! o'er death and hell He reigneth
  Bursting back the gates of doom !

III

Manifold the attestation :
  Brethren tell the marvel o'er,
And the soldiers from their station,
  And the angels at the door,
And His Own Word's revelation,
  'Lo ! I live for evermore.'

IV

Now He lives and reigns for ever
  That we too may enter in
Where eternal life shall never
  Taste of sorrow or of sin,
Where from Him no death shall sever
  Those He vanquished death to win.

V

Saviour ! in *our* night of weeping
  Tell us of the joyful morn,
Guard our souls, their vigil keeping,
  In the hours of hate and scorn ;
Raise us falling, wake us sleeping,
  Till *our* Easter Day be born.   Amen.

The Ascension

' He ascended into heaven, and sitteth on the right hand of
God the Father Almighty.'

I

On Olivet a little band
Around their risen Master stand :
And, after charge and blessing given,
He passeth from them into Heaven.

II

Wistful their eyes, but angels twain
Cheer them with glorious words : ' Again
One day shall Jesus even so
Return, as ye have seen Him go.'

III

Till then in Heaven He doth remain,
True God, at God's right hand to reign,
True Man, at human woes to grieve,
True God, Almighty to relieve.

IV

For every soul in every need
He ever lives to intercede,
Presenting there within the veil
The Sacrifice that cannot fail.

V

Our heavenly great High Priest He stands :
By piercèd Feet, and piercèd Hands,
By thorn-scarr'd Brow and riven Side,
He pleads for those for whom He died !

VI

Whom have we, LORD, in heaven but thee ?
Like ships safe moored on stormy sea
Our souls, in peril, with Thee there
Find anchorage of hope and prayer.

VII

Set loose from earth, and evermore
Fast bound to that eternal shore,
So all our life and love shall be,
Ascended Master, hid with Thee !　　Amen.

The Judgment

'He shall come to judge the quick and the dead.'

I

WISTFUL are our waiting eyes,
As of them who saw Him rise
From that mountain to the skies.

II

Then the holy angels near
Gave them tidings of good cheer:
'JESUS shall again appear.'

III

And *we* wait an angel's cry,
Piercing earthward from the sky:
'Now, behold, your LORD is nigh!'

IV

Yet who shall abide that day,
When the Judge with dread array
Comes for universal sway?

V

Dreadful shall His summons sweep,
Heard by those who wake or sleep,
On the height or in the deep:

T

VI

Heard by life 'mid all its bloom,
Heard by death in every tomb—
Terrible decree of doom.

VII

As the fisher parts his prey,
Casting these from those away,
So it shall be on that day.

VIII

For the gathered souls who stand,
Waiting that supreme command,
He shall part on either hand.

IX

To those souls of quick and dead,
'Come,' shall be the blessing said,
'Go,' shall be the cursing dread.

X

LORD, dwell in us now, we pray,
That, in the dividing day,
We be not the cast away!

XI

So shall we till Thou appear
Blend, in longing eye and ear,
Holy joy with holy fear!   Amen.

The Resurrection of the Body

I

WINTER in his heart of gloom
Sings the songs of coming bloom :
So o'er death our souls shall sing
Lays of the eternal spring.

II

Then decay shall be no more,
And the weary seed-time o'er,
All the dead in CHRIST shall rise
For the harvest of the skies.

III

Wheresoe'er the faithful sleep
Angels shall go forth to reap,
From the dust and 'neath the foam
They shall bring the harvest home.

IV

Bodies of the saints, whose bones
Rest beneath sepulchral stones,
Or are lost on every wind—
All, those messengers shall find.

V

All from earth to heaven shall soar
In that flesh which once they wore,
Deathless now and glorified,
Like their LORD and at His side.

VI

This is life's eternal spring !
This the coming joy we sing !
Look we ever towards this day,
Be it near or far away !

VII

'Mid the sorrow and the strife
'Tis the music of our life,
And the song hath this refrain—
Our Redeemer comes again !   Amen.

The Life Everlasting

I

THE world is sad with hopes that die,
With joys that gleam and then go by,
And dim the mortal eyes that gaze
On setting suns of parting days.

II

Better the hope, the joy, the light,
For spiritual heart and sight!
For they whose life is hid on high
Shall never part and never die.

III

They never part! that saintly band,
Heirs of the heavenly, holy land;
Whom GOD the SPIRIT hath made one
With GOD the FATHER and the SON.

IV

They never die ! the deathly strife
But ushers them to happier life :
From their last enemy they gain
Their birth to bliss, their end to pain.

V

LORD JESU, teach our hearts to soar
And grasp those things which are before,
That after death our life may be
The immortality with Thee !   Amen.

Note.—It will be seen that the preceding ten Hymns are on the several Articles of the Apostles' Creed. The two omitted here—' *The Church's One Foundation*,' on ' The Holy Catholic Church,' and ' *Weary of Earth and laden with my Sin*,' on ' The Forgiveness of Sins '—are printed in the Author's former volume, *The Knight of Intercession.*

Christmas Carol

I

While the shepherds kept their vigil,
    And the world in darkness lay,
Came the holy Advent Angel;
    Shone the sudden glory ray;
Then, ten thousand times ten thousand
    Radiant heralds of the day.

II

Then they sang the first sweet carol,
    'Glory be to God on high,
And on earth be peace and blessing
    To the nations far and nigh!'
So our God made good His promise,
    And the old prophetic cry.

III

Fuller, farther o'er the wide world,
    Year by year that music swells;
Year by year to some new people
    Christmastide the story tells—
With the chanting of the children,
    And the pealing of the bells.

IV

Louder over hill and valley
　　Let the towers and steeples ring !
In the hamlet and the city
　　Sweeter carols let us sing—
Louder peals of holy pleasure,
　　Sweeter carols to our King.

V

Hear Thy children, blessed JESUS,
　　Once for us on earth a Child ;
Keep us in Thy great compassion,
　　Holy, harmless, undefiled ;
Blest through Thee by GOD the SPIRIT,
　　To the FATHER reconciled.

VI

Still we look for thine appearing,
　　O Thou Bright and Morning Star !
Still we wait to hear the rolling
　　Of Thy great triumphal car ;—
We who sing Thy first glad Advent,
　　Know Thy second is not far.　　Amen.

Hymn for the Lord's Day

I

EASTWARD, ever eastward,
  Dark or light the way,
Pressing towards the promise,
  We salute the day.
O'er the mountains yonder
  Shines the orient gleam,
Yonder sweetest voices
  Call across the stream.

Eastward, ever eastward,
  Dark or light the way,
Pressing towards the promise,
  We salute the day.

II

To those border mountains
  Lift we then our eyes:
Thence our help smiles on us,
  There is set our Prize—

There, like sound of trumpet,
  Clear, and loud, and long,
Easter splendour streaming
  Greets our Easter song.

III

Flow life's river cheerly—
  Flow it dark and chill—
O'er its changeful waters
  Constant look we still.
Clear across them beckons
  The unchanging shore,
Where the life and beauty
  Are for evermore.

IV

Saints and angels call us—
  Angels of the height,
Who at Incarnation
  Sang the new-born light :
Saints gone on before us,
  Past our life forlorn,
Who in Eden's Vigil
  Wait the greater Morn.

V

Death of woful winter !
  Dawn of happy spring !
Listen, all the woodlands
  Of the wide world ring !
Look, the waste lands blossom
  'Neath the gracious rain,
And all beauty buried
  Takes its life again !

VI

Oh, the end of patience,
  And the close of strife !
Oh, the joy of morning,
  And the gift of life !
Oh, the grace, the glory,
  Of the great Reward !
Oh, the blessed Vision,
  JESUS CHRIST our LORD !

Eastward, ever eastward,
  Dark or light the way,
Pressing towards the promise,
  We salute the day.   Amen.

Hymn of Unity

PART I

(EPH. iv. 6 and 13)

I

God the Father, All, and One,
With the SPIRIT, and the SON,
Make and keep us one in Thee,
O Eternal Unity !

II

Over all, through all, in all,
FATHER-GOD, to Thee we call :
By Thine all-embracing plan
Bring us to the perfect man.

III

To the perfect man of truth
Wise as age and sweet as youth ;
To the perfect man of love
One with Him, our Head above.   Amen.

PART II

I

Of true union only Power
For the age or for the hour,
SPIRIT, with Thee make us one
In the FATHER and the SON.

II

In one Body one on earth,
By one spiritual Birth;
One in sevenfold gifts from heaven
E'en as Thou, the ONE, art Seven.

III

One in mind and word and will,
One at war with all of ill,
One in peace amid the strife,
One in sweetest hope of life.

IV

One in patience of to-day,
One in future bliss for aye:
In the FATHER, SON, and Thee
One to all eternity.   Amen.

PART III

I

Only Saviour, Prince of Peace,
Bid our long dissensions cease :
Show us in our own self-will
Deeper danger, surest ill.

II

JESUS, lowly may we be,
Strong in gentleness like Thee ;
Nobly meek as sternly pure :
Strong to do and to endure.

III

Teach us of the cross we bear—
Of the crown that we shall wear—
Of our will for Thee laid low—
Of the glory we shall know.

IV

Of the waiting and the pain,
Of the more exceeding gain—
Pain, our loyal hearts to prove,
Gain, the triumph of our Love.   Amen.

Hymn for Day and Sunday School Teachers[1]

I

THOU who hast charged Thine elder sons,
  In Thy great Church's school
To teach and tend Thy little ones,
  And in wise love to rule:
Here may they loyal witness bear,
  As those whom Thou hast sent,
By Love inspired, kept pure by Prayer,
  Made strong by Sacrament.

II

And ever here, LORD CHRIST, be seen
  Standing beneath Thy Rood,
Stoled in Thy raiment, white and clean,
  A priestly sisterhood;
Which in Thy Church's order sure
  May in the dark world shine
Like her, the wise, the brave, the pure,
  Their own Saint Katharine.

[1] Adapted from a Hymn written by the Author for the Church Training College of St. Katharine, Tottenham.

III

Teacher of teachers, only Guide,
  True learning's only spring,
O HOLY GHOST, with each abide,
  All truth interpreting;
From light to light of mind and soul,
  And pure, devoted will,
Lead on Thy learners to the goal
  Of wisdom's holy hill.

IV

Lead on, O LORD—Love, Grace, and Might—
  Lead on through toil and prayer;
So worship shall make labour light,
  And hope ennoble care;
So they adoring while they toil,
  Their guerdon may foresee,
When at Thy feet they lay the spoil
  Of souls they trained for Thee.   Amen.

Hymn for Church Workers

'I magnify mine office.'—(ROM. xi. 13)

I

LORD CHRIST, my Master dear,
Nought have I that is mine;
Body and mind and soul,
All that I am is Thine.

II

Mine office is from Thee:
Not only for mine hour,
But for Thine own great day,
And by Thy mighty power.

III

Through Thine own Church it comes,
From Thine Ascension Day,
By Thine ordaining word
Which cannot pass away.

IV

So do I love Thy call!
So great and sweet to me
U

That word which makes me sure
That I may speak for Thee.

v

How poor am I in love,
In patience, and in power,
Yet more than I can be
Is, by that word, my dower!

VI

Power, patience, love, are mine,
From Thee, my Priest on high,
If I in faith and prayer
Mine office magnify.

VII

For, then, I lose myself!
I know it is not mine;
Thereon I see the mark
Which makes it wholly Thine:

VIII

Thy Cross, Incarnate LORD!
The measure of Thy love,
Of Thy great power below,
Of Thy full bliss above.   Amen.

Hymn of All Angels

I

Lo, they were, and they are, and shall be,
    Ere the world, in the world, to the end !
For their LORD, for His Church, and for me,
    Each a minister, guardian, and friend.

II

They were all of the covenants twain ;
    Both before and from Sinai, the host
Serving GOD in their courses, the train
    Of JEHOVAH, the One HOLY GHOST.

III

And throughout the more excellent way,
    Both before and from Zion, they wrought :
Poets, prophets, and ministers they
    Of the grace the unpriced, the unbought.

IV

For they sang of Emmanuel's birth,
    As they sang at the morning of time,
Of the peace for this woe-stricken earth
    Coming down from the glory sublime.

V

They were His in His pain and His power,
   In Gethsemane's uttermost gloom,
E'en as in the all-conquering hour
   When He shattered the gates of His doom.

VI

They were theirs whom He sent to His war
   To o'erthrow and recover His world ;
And so still they are flying afar
   With the flag that His saints have unfurled.

VII

They are with us in vigil alway,
   All above us, beneath, at our side,
And our souls they shall reap at the day
   Of the Master's supreme Harvest-tide.

VIII

Then, O FATHER of Angels, shall we
   Sing to Thee with that infinite host ;
And, O Covenant ANGEL, to Thee,
   And to Thee, O Thou One HOLY GHOST.

Amen.

Four Hymns of St. Thomas à Kempis

(Paraphrased from the Latin)

Hymn I

De Trinitate

I

Most true, most High: O Trinity,
Equal and undivided Three!
Our lauds of honour, power and praise
And victory, unto Thee we raise.

II

With mind and heart on Thee we call:
Our knees before Thy footstool fall:
Our hands we lift in fervent prayer:
Our voices all Thy praise declare.

III

Creator! Who to us hast given
The earth, the ocean, and the heaven:
From Thee too comes our joy of heart:
Our way, and truth, and life Thou art.

IV

Thee all things praise; in Thee they move,
All things below and all above:
The secret things of deepest Hell,
Not hid to Thee, Thine honour tell.

V

O FATHER, Thine the glory be,
Such glory, only SON, to Thee:
And unto Thee, Whom we adore,
The PARACLETE, for evermore.　　Amen.

HYMN II

De Dulcedine Jesu

'Unto you which believe He is precious.'—(1 PET. ii. 7.)

I

JESU, to my heart most precious,
　　Who didst leave Thy Heaven above,
To the lost world the Life-giver!
　　O that I my love may prove,
Read, and sing, and tell Thy story,
　　Theme of sweetness, song of Love!

II

He who leaves Thee—Oh, the sorrow!
  He who finds Thee—Oh, the bliss!
For the LORD of Earth and Heaven
  Shall for evermore be His:
Who (O marvel!) chose the manger,
  And gave up that world for this!

III

These delights—the best and sweetest
  To the faithful soul must be—
To recall Thee, O my Saviour,
  In Thy great Humility!
In Thine absence these the relics,
  Holiest, dearest unto me!

IV

I am glad—one time in anguish:
  I, one time so blind, can see:
Unto me in darksome prison
  JESUS came, and I am free!
Naked, foolish, languid, dying—
  Heaven's Physician came to me!

V

FATHER of all light and goodness,
  Thou hast loved me in His grace :
For in Him Thou hast provided
  From the storms a hiding-place.
JESU, every cure of sadness
  Is reflected in Thy Face.

VI

Praise to Thee, my kindest Saviour,
  Thee, my LORD and GOD for aye ;
I am Thine, to my rejoicing,
  Till the world shall pass away :
By Thy Love, O make me love Thee
  More and more as day by day.   Amen.

HYMN III

EVENING

O qualis, quantaque Lætitia

PART I

'Angels and men in a wonderful order.'

I

O JOY, the purest, noblest,
That fills the heavenly land,
Of JESUS and His chosen
And all th' angelic band :
Glad faces and sweet voices
Round the Creator's throne,
Adore Him, give Him glory,
Their love and homage own.

II

There with the peal of trumpets
And thrilling harp-notes clear,
In raiment white and glistering,
The Angel hosts appear.
There on swift wing of service,
Or waiting His command,
In the Thrice Holy Presence,
They ever speed or stand.

III

There 'HOLY, HOLY, HOLY'—
    The better country's song—
Quells every sound of sorrow,
    Of weeping and of wrong :
There every voice in concord,
    There every heart in tune,
Intent in rapture, worships
    The Blessed THREE IN ONE.

IV

The Cherubs and the Seraphs
    In love and praise adore ;
Praise that is never-ceasing,
    Love that is more and more :
Thrones, virtues, and dominions,
    Powers, principalities,
Heaven's highest good enjoying
    In love that never dies.

V

The Angels and Archangels,
    Rejoicing in the height,
For all—the high or lowly—
    In watchful care delight ;

To GOD they bear our praises,
  From GOD His gifts they bring;
They comfort, guide us, guard us,
  And while they serve they sing

VI

These are we fain to honour,
  These are we fain to love;
With heart and life and utterance
  Fixed on these things above:
There in the blissful regions
  Of that all-beauteous land
Where men elect with Angels
  Shall make one glorious band.   Amen.

PART II

I

State of divinest splendour!
  Home of all perfect rest!
With peace in all Thy borders,
  With light of beauty blest;
The citizens within thee
  In purest raiment shine,
And keep, in union closest,
  The law of love Divine.

II

Nought is there that they know not :
  Their service is not toil :
There never comes temptation,
  Nor earthly care or moil ;
There they are ever happy :
  There they are ever wise :
There is their lot o'erflowing
  With all that satisfies.

III

O sweet and blest communion ;
  Love, Holiness, Truth, Light !
Where reigns the Triune Godhead
  In blessing infinite.
To Him be praise and honour
  From Angels and from men,
Whose grace this glory gave us :
  Blessed be GOD !   Amen.

Hymn IV

PATIENCE

De Patientia Servanda

I

Bear the troubles of thy life
  In the name of Christ thy Lord:
Less the harm of stormy strife
  Than the easy world's award.

II

Many a foe means many a friend;
  Earthly losing is not loss;
Patience has her perfect end,
  And all good flows from the Cross.

III

Small thy toil is: short thy life:
  Grand and endless thy reward!
Through the sorrow and the strife,
  The confession of thy Lord!

IV

Purer gold and clearer glass!
  By thy pains a nobler man,
Through the furnace thou wilt pass,
  Bearing all a martyr can.

V

So thou wilt be sterner foe,
  So thou wilt be dearer friend;
So the Saints thy name will know,
  And CHRIST own thee at the end.

VI

Call on JESUS evermore,
  Be His Cross thy sign alway,
Love the saints gone on before;
  Ever strive and watch and pray.

VII

Do the right: the truth declare!
  Live in hopes that never cease:
Humbly make thy GOD thy care,
  So thou shalt find perfect peace.   Amen.

Follow On: An Epiphany Carol

' Then shall we know, if we follow on to know the Lord.'
(HOSEA vi. 3.)

I

THE Epiphany Star, the CHRIST's ensign afar,
    Shone clear o'er the cradle of morn ;
And a musical wind, from the darkness behind,
    Breathed soft o'er the desert forlorn,
    Breathed soft o'er the desert forlorn ;
Like the song that is sung by a glad mother's tongue
    When her child of travail is born.

Refrain :

    Follow on, follow on, till the night is gone :
    Till the long hard quest has its end in rest,
    And the vision of CHRIST is won.

II

Now arise thou and shine ! for this signal is thine,
    O world sitting sad in the gloom !

On thy longing and prayer, on thine utter despair,
　　Gross darkness has lain like a doom,
　　Gross darkness has lain like a doom ;
But thy mourning is done, and an unsetting sun
　　Thy life shall for ever illume.

III

Take your garments of praise, and your carols upraise,
　　O Continent, City, and Isle !
Flow together and sing—with the subject the king—
　　Together ye waited long while,
　　Together ye waited long while ;
With a wonderful bloom, like a soul from the tomb,
　　The universe desert shall smile !

IV

O'er the dreary sand sea, sped the King Sages three
　　As they listened that mystic lay ;
And serene on their sight fell the marvellous light,
　　CHRIST's sign set in Heaven, alway,
　　CHRIST's sign set in Heaven, alway ;
Never star, never moon, never splendour of noon,
　　Shone like the Epiphany ray.

V

So in trust did they fare, thro’ long peril and care,
    O’er that great and terrible wild ;
Till, enrapt on the face of CHRIST’s infinite grace
    On the breast of His Mother mild,
    On the breast of His Mother mild ;
Upon them from His eyes, deeper depths than the
    skies,
    The One Light of the whole world smiled.

VI

Kneeling low they outpoured their trine gifts to the
    LORD,
    As he royally blest them there ;
Gold and Myrrh at His feet, and the Frankincense
    sweet,
    Their Charity, Penitence, Prayer,
    Their Charity, Penitence, Prayer ;
To the Monarch Most High, to the Man who must
    die,
    To their GOD was this tribute rare.

VII

Follow ! so follow on, Christians every one,
    Hold the hope of your patience fast

X

Till the Day-star arise, and your happy eyes
　　See the King in Beauty at last,
　　See the King in Beauty at last;
And the Love, Work, and Praise of your pilgrimage
　　days
　　At the feet of your LORD are cast.

Refrain:
　　Follow on, follow on, till the night is gone:
　　Till the long hard quest has its end in rest,
　　And the vision of CHRIST is won.

𝔐arriage 𝔥ymn

'God the Father, God the Son, God the Holy Ghost,
bless, preserve, and keep you.'

(Office of Holy Matrimony.)

I

O Thou, Whose love paternal,
　Ere yet had entered in
On Eden's beauty vernal
　The wintry curse of sin,
In bonds of blessing golden
　Did join the primal twain,
That benediction olden,
　O Father, grant again !

II

O Christ, Whose love for ever,
　Strong as eternity,
Hath willed that nought should sever
　Thy holy Church and Thee;
Oh, by that great Communion
　That none shall e'er divide,
Be here to bless this union,
　This Bridegroom and this Bride !

III

Spirit of peace and gladness,
  Whose holy presence given
Can make this world of sadness
  The border-land of Heaven;
O Leader and Defender!
  Be theirs—to guard and guide,
Now in life's mid-day splendour,
  On to the even-tide!

IV

O Trinal Power and Glory!
  O Undivided Three!
Grant that these twain before Thee
  Be ever one in Thee!
One *now* in ways of Duty
  Made bright by holy love,
One *then* in Bliss and Beauty
  Eternally above!   Amen.

The Proto-Martyr of Britain: A Hymn in Memory of St. Alban

DEDICATED TO A. C. S. AND M. S. S.

'Egregium Albanum fœcunda Britannia profert.'
> (*Venantius Fortunatus.*   Fifth Century.)

'Thus was Alban tried,
England's first Martyr, whom no threats could shake;
Self-offered victim; for his friend he died,
And for the Faith.'   (WORDSWORTH.)

The story of the Saint as we have it from Bede and other sources is shortly this :—He was the wealthy and cultured heir of a Roman house, and lived at Verulam, in Hertfordshire, about the year 280 A.D.   A hunted Christian priest sought refuge in his house.   His intercourse with this fugitive led to his conversion and baptism.   The author of *Martyrs and Saints of the First Twelve Centuries* (S.P.C.K) says admirably that the priest 'attracted him by no seductive promises: it was the old trumpet-call to believe and follow, to sacrifice and suffer, which penetrates so much deeper, and leads so much higher.'   This has suggested the refrain of this hymn.   Alban after his baptism saved the life of this priest at the sacrifice of his own.   He was brought before the Roman judge, and, after having been tortured, he was beheaded on June 22nd, A.D. 283.

I

ENGLAND, by thine own Saint Alban,

  Put thy Christian heart to school:

Learn to sacrifice and suffer

  By thy Proto-Martyr's rule.

Life in CHRIST is stern and selfless,

  Gentle though it be and bright:

Life in CHRIST is dying with Him,
　Though in sweet and living light.
　　England, by thine own Saint Alban,
　　　Put thy Christian heart to school :
　　Learn to sacrifice and suffer
　　　By thy Proto-Martyr's rule.

II

Meteor-like athwart the darkness
　Flashes still the Signal Cross ;
Still like trumpet on the night-wind
　Sounds the summons unto loss ;
Yet how blessed is the losing,
　And how stately is the war :
And how beautiful the ending
　In the bliss for evermore !

III

See ! thy hero, prudence scorning,
　All for noble pity dares :
Finds the priest he saved his prophet,
　Meets ' an angel unawares ' :
Sits as at the feet of JESUS,
　Soon is to His Laver led :
Then himself as on an altar
　Offers in his Teacher's stead.

IV

'I am CHRIST'S : I therefore suffer :
   I am CHRIST'S : I therefore die :
I am CHRIST'S : so I am happy,
   And my life is His on high ';—
Thus he faced the Roman's torture,
   Youth, wealth, honour sacrificed,
Losing thankfully the whole world
   That he might be found in CHRIST.

V

Primal Hero-Saint and Soldier !
   Still thy story speeds us on :
Though, since thou did'st bravely witness,
   Twice eight hundred years have gone.
LORD, Who gavest him to England,
   Grace, like his, to England give—
Grace to bear Thy cross with gladness,
   Grace to die that we may live.

   England, by thine own Saint Alban,
      Put thy Christian heart to school :
   Learn to sacrifice and suffer
      By thy Proto-Martyr's rule.   Amen.

Rogation Hymn

I

FATHER, we pray through Him Who went by pain
  To bliss, nor won His glory ere He died;
We pray, as seeing the High-priestly reign
  Of Him, th' Ascended, once the Crucified :—
So ever for all help in all our need
The Offering, thus made perfect, now we plead.

II

We pray 'midst the convulsions of a life
  Of sad necessities, of pains, of fears,
'Midst the long hours of spiritual strife
  Which make the wild or melancholy years;
But 'midst all stress or storm one Hope we own,
Faith's Beacon, our High Priest before Thy Throne!

III

Oh, we have sinned! ill deed, unholy thought,
  Abuse of speech Thou gavest us for praise,
Kind words unsaid, sweet charities unwrought,
  Unheeded grace, unconsecrated days :

Self-love, and selfish mood, and wayward will,—
These haunt our souls with memories of ill.

IV

Oh, we have sinned ! but since He loved so well
   The souls Thy love predestined Him to gain,
Help us to front our fears of death and hell,
   And by the Blood which was not spilt in vain,
And by the open Tomb, and opened Sky,
Assure our hearts that Thou wilt hear their cry.

V

The inward cry for mercy, grace, and peace,
   From hearts that know the secret plague within ;
Longings for Purity, for Faith's increase,
   More love of Truth, a truer hate of sin ;
More Patience and more power to persevere ;
To be more like our LORD—to be more near.

VI

Nor less, O LORD, through Him Who intercedes,
   We bear upon our hearts before Thee those
Bent low by this world's miseries or needs,
   The martyrs of its sins or of its woes ;
And all whose lives are hidden—the unknown,
Except for Thee forgotten and alone.

VII

FATHER, we plead, too, for our own dear land,
   Its threefold Motherhood, its triple Home,
Hearth, Country, Church: from which Thy great
      command
   With promise bids our true faith never roam:
To each Thy peace, to each Thy power impart—
Pure love, clear sight, strong hand, and loyal heart.

VIII

And last, we humbly claim Thy power and grace
   For those who lead Thy wars in all the world:
Thy toilers in all climes, of every race,
   Warring till sin and death he overhurled.
By Him Who died, but lives to plead on high,
For these, for all, Our FATHER, hear our cry.　Amen.

A Hymn of the Sea

The inroad of the sea upon the Norfolk coast, near Cromer, made it necessary some two years ago to remove the Church of Sidestrand and to rebuild it further inland. This hymn was written for use at the first service after this change.

In the hymn the Sea represents Time, by which God speaks; the removal of the Fabric inland represents the passing of the Spiritual Church in the course of Time to the Peace of Paradise; until it shall pass by another change to the final Glory of Heaven, where 'there will be no more Sea,' for 'there shall be Time no longer.'

I

Lord of all, beside Thy Sea
Lift we prayer and praise to Thee;
Thine we were, and Thine we are,
By Thy waters near or far.

II

Near Thy Sea our Church-bell tolled
And, beneath, the breakers rolled;
And the toll became a dirge,
Chiming with the solemn surge.

III

Long the billows moaned in fear,
'Church of God, the time is near':
Then, full-toned, like voice of doom,
'Rise and go, the End is come.'

IV

So Thy near Sea sang its knell;
Yet Thou workest all things well;
Inland at Thy will we move,
Knowing that Thy will is love.

V

So we pass away in peace,
Where our fears and perils cease;
Where the voice of praise and prayer
Rises in serener air.

VI

Yet Thy far Sea still is heard:
From its great deep rolls the word,
'Church in vigil, wait and pray,
Thou again shalt pass away.'

VII

Voice of Time, prophetic Sea !
Speaking, Lord of all, for Thee ;
So its message shoreward rolls—
Poet-Preacher unto souls.

VIII

Give us grace to hear and heed,
That we may be Thine indeed—
That to us in turn be given
Earth and Paradise and Heaven.

IX

Earth : till from Time's roaring strand
We must seek the Quiet Land,
Till the farther waters say,
' Lo, the kingdom ! come away.'

X

JESU, Thine we were and are,
By Thy waters near and far ;
Oh, may we be still in Thee
When there shall be no more Sea !   Amen.

Hymn after Holy Communion

' Ye do show the Lord's Death.'—(1 COR. xi. 26.)
"Jesus said, Somebody hath touched Me ; for I perceive that
virtue is gone out of Me.'—(ST. LUKE viii. 46.)

I

Now hath been shown, O LORD, Thine Act of Love :
Shown at Thine Altar here, and shown above.

II

Here hath been pleaded, and beyond the skies,
The perfect yet perpetual Sacrifice.

III

Thou hast been with us, and in very deed
From Thee hath virtue gone for all our need :

IV

Pardon and Peace and Joy : the making whole,
The making glad, of every faithful soul.

V

How dared we come so close despite our fear?
Because we knew the LORD of Love was near.

VI

Thou camest—through the midst of many a care,
The mind's depression or the soul's despair—

VII

A Presence calm—in awful silence—known,
By healing touch, to those in need alone.

VIII

Then Thou didst bless us !   Now, O LORD, we pray
May this Thy Grace grow in us day by day :   ·

IX

Thy Grace of Meekness, learned beneath Thy Feet,
Where all things strong with all things lowly meet ;

X

Thy Grace of Faith, serene and open-eyed,
Far-gazing, till it shall be satisfied ;

XI

Thy Grace of Zeal, in toil or patience sure,
Keen to press on, or happy to endure ;

XII

Thy Grace of Love, the purest, noblest, best,
With eyes on Thee and trustful heart at rest.

XIII

Thy Grace of Joy, for ever fain to sing
The Praise of Thine Eternal Offering.   Amen.

Sudden Death

'From sudden death, Good Lord, deliver us.'
                                        (*The Litany.*)

I

WHEN our last soul-calling
    Comes, LORD, at Thy will,
Grant there be no falling
    'Neath the lord of ill—
No swift, subtle capture
    By our ghostly foe
E'en if sudden rapture
    Wing us from our woe.

II

Should he find us sleeping
    In or sloth or pride,
No stern vigil keeping
    Staunch at every tide;
Should the city's taking
    Be its warriors' blame,
O the wild up-waking
    To eternal shame !

III

Jesu, save, in pity,
    From such dread surprise
Each soul of that city
    Precious in Thine eyes.
Swiftly then, or slowly—
    Comes no end amiss—
May Thine angel holy
    Call us into bliss.

IV

Death will be that angel,
    Saviour, of Thy will,
With the same evangel,
    Jubilant or still;
Crowning toilsome duty
    And long years of pain,
Or youth's joy and beauty,
    With exceeding gain:

V

Death, all slowly brightening
    Some gloom-haunted way;
Y

Death, as instant lightning
  On meridian day—
Welcome !—if Thou meet us,
  Lord, when he shall come,
And Thy dear saints greet us
  To our Father's Home.   Amen.

The Beating Down of Satan

'We beseech Thee . . . finally to beat down Satan under our feet.'—(*The Litany.*)

'For He must reign till He hath put all enemies under His feet.'

(1 COR. xv. 25.)

I

WATCHING early, late, and long,
Sworn to crown his work of wrong,
Satan would our doom complete,
Tread us down beneath his feet.

II

CHRIST against him aid us well!—
When fair lures lead on to hell;
While the Spring blows free and fresh,—
LORD, beat down the lust of flesh.

III

When our life in Summer noon,
Reigning through its roseate June,
Seems an age that cannot die,—
LORD, beat down the lust of eye.

IV

When the golden Autumn throws
Glory on a proud repose,
Or adorns a splendid strife,—
LORD, beat down the pride of life.

V

When, with Death, at Winter's night,
He shall come in Hope's despite,
And all powers and passions fleet,—
Beat him down beneath our feet.

VI

Thou, Whose love hath made us free,
When he claims us finally
At the dread tribunal seat,—
Beat him down beneath our feet.   Amen.

Sent: A Hymn for Candidates for Ordination

' Who is sufficient for these things.'
' Even so send I you.'

I

O MY LORD, most Holy,
  Summonest Thou me,
Lowliest 'mid the lowly,
  As Thyself to be?
' *Yea, because I call thee,*
  Take thy priestly place,
Front what may befall thee—
  Hast thou not My grace?'

II

Can I in my weakness
  Stand as in Thy stead?
I, in might or meekness,
  Needing to be led?
'*Yes, for I have sent thee,*
  Laid on thee My power;
Be, by what is lent thee,
  Equal to thine hour.'

III

How may I be leader,
　　Doubting mine own way?
Of Thy flock the feeder,
　　Oft myself astray?
' Canst not trust thy Master
　　His elect to keep?
Think, 'tis thine own Pastor
　　Set thee o'er His sheep.'

IV

LORD, who can awaken
　　Israel cold and dead,
Now that Thou art taken
　　From Thy Church's head?
' Lo, My mantle folds thee
　　From My car of fire!
Mine Ascension holds thee
　　With Me to aspire.

V

' Canst thou fear or falter
　　Clothed with such a claim?
Standing at Mine Altar,
　　Blessing in My Name?

When Life's path grows steeper,
Pointing out the Height,
'Mid the darkness deeper
Holding out the light.'

VI

O my Master, truly
  Thou hast met my need !
They who follow duly
  Duly Thine may lead ;
Following Thee for ever,
  As Thou wilt and where,
I, in Thee, will never
  Falter or despair.

VII

FATHER, SON, and SPIRIT,
  'Tis Thy call of grace,
Thine election's merit
  Seals to me my place :
Lowest 'mid the lowly,
  Yet I call Thee mine :
HOLY, HOLY, HOLY,
  Thine, and sent to Thine.   Amen.

The Stream of Time: A New Year's Hymn

I

OUT of silence, fateful,
　　Flows the Stream of years ;
In its mystery hateful,
　　Brooded o'er by fears.
' O faint heart, above it
　　See th' o'erwatching sky ;
For life's mystery love it,
　　On its hope rely !'

II

But this sky of morning
　　Dark may be ere noon ;
All my fond hope scorning,
　　Be it late or soon.
' Nay, that Heaven remaineth,
　　Come the clouds or go ;
Evermore it reigneth
　　O'er the River's flow.'

III

Say, what room for gladness,
　　While these waters moan ?

Infinite in sadness
  Is this river's tone.
' *All emotions blending*
  To its course belong ;
But of joy unending
  Is its undersong !

IV

' *Fear not !*   *He Who made it*
  Is thine own true Friend ;
For thy sake He bade it
  Flow from source to end.
His own Heaven its fountain,
  To His deep it flows ;
Springing from love's Mountain,
  Love is its repose.

V

' *Yea ; and He before thee,*
  On this river's breast,
Passed from pain to glory,
  Passed from toil to rest.
Follow, till He meet thee—
  Down this narrow tide—
Till His smile shall greet thee
  On His Ocean wide.'   *Amen.*

Hymn of All Hallows

'O love the Lord, all ye His saints.'—(PS. xxxi. 23.)
'Lo, a great multitude.'—(REV. vii. 9.)

I

ALL HALLOWS : by that voice Deep calls to Deep :
    Altar to Altar : Word replies to Word ;
They throng the plain, and vale, and crown the steep—
    Earth, Hades, Heaven—in each their sound is
        heard.
All tones therein of grace and glory blend,
GOD's love in purpose, and GOD's love in end.

II

All Hallows : evermore from age to age
    The meek, majestic, loyal line goes on ;
Their pictures front us on each holy page—
    From primal Genesis to mystic John ;
With myriads more on those blank leaves between
By reverent angels marked, by men unseen.

III

All Hallows : Abel at his altar stands ;
   Noah, and Abraham, and Aaron, there ;
Each dimly gazing, Crosswards, to those Hands
   Which all men's sins and all men's sorrows bear ;
And to that Precious Stream, from Calvary's height,
Wherein All Hallows wash their raiment white.

IV

All Hallows : these are they redeemed by love :
   Elect by GOD the FATHER to be won
By Him He gave : sealed by the mystic DOVE
   Who lit on them, as on th' Incarnate SON,
To make them His—the pure, the kind, the true,
The brave to suffer and the strong to do.

V

LORD of All Hallows,—of that multitude,
   The stoled in white who sing before Thy throne,
Where never pain may dull, nor pride delude
   Those happy spirits evermore thine own ;
Grant us their faith and patience—and their love,
Their power below, in Thee, their bliss above.

Amen.

Hymn after Benediction

I

HOMEWARD we pass, in Peace :
 Our Master's message given :
He sends us on our earthly way
 With words from Heaven.

II

The Church's words are His :
 This ' Peace ' is said with power ;
His Blood-bought Blessing is her charge,
 Her children's dower.

III

To every faithful soul
 There at the Altar stand
The Love, Grace, Might, of GOD TRIUNE,
 With lifted hand.

IV

Hear tender Mercy's words,
  Ye souls that inly mourn!
Receive your Saviour's Sympathy,
    Ye hearts forlorn!

V

Hear Wisdom's word of light,
  All ye who long to find
The knowledge that can free and fill
    The troubled mind.

VI

So blest in mind and heart
  Homeward we pass to-day:
Dear LORD, so may we wend at last
    Our Heavenward way.   Amen.

The Three Homes

(For Very Young Children)

I

God is so good : He gives us Home,
　And all in Home so dear :
And till we to His kingdom come,
　He makes us happy here.

II

Another Home He gives us too :
　That Home the Church we call ;
To her we will be ever true,
　The Mother of us all.

III

And still another does He give !
　Wherever we may roam,
Wherever British children live,
　Their country is their Home.

IV

And in that Home a great Queen dwells
In royal motherhood—
Ring out her name, ye merry bells,
Victoria the Good !

V

We praise God for our Mother-Queen,
Tender and true is she ;
A greater there has never been—
A kinder could not be.

VI

So while the bells ring out her fame,
Our song of praise to Thee
We children chant, in JESUS' name,
Most Holy Trinity.   Amen.

God of Supreme Dominion

HYMN OF THE DIAMOND WEDDING OF THE QUEEN
WITH HER PEOPLE

' The Diamond Wedding of the Queen with her people.'—(*Times*
Leader, *Nov.* 10, 1896.)

' It is a full song that will greet the Diamond Marriage Year of
the Queen with her people; going up from the "silver-coasted"
Islands of Britain; from the golden Australasian Islands : from
the sunny Islands of the Tropics : from the Indian Empire, from
Africa, from the darker Canadian North, and from many another
land.'

I

GOD of supreme dominion,
    From Whom all power has birth,
Whose Praise on eagle pinion
    O'ersweeps Thine Heav'n and earth :
We lift one voice before Thee
    From many a land and race,
And with one heart adore Thee
    For threescore years of grace.

II

Here, by the barriers olden
    With front of silver sheen—

There, from the Islands golden—
From Orient lands between—
From isles of beauty sparkling
The summer seas among—
From tracts with winter darkling—
Goes up the choral song.

III

These years, in tale excelling
All years of olden reign,
Their twofold story telling
Of blended joy and pain—
With equal grace upon her,
Like twain wings of Thy Dove—
Have crowned the Head we honour:
Have blessed the Heart we love.

IV

Comes with prophetic morning,
With Peace afar and near,
With Hope our hills adorning,
This Diamond Marriage Year!
And hearts with praise o'erflowing,
And souls that inly pray,

Greet Queen and Nation going
　Still on their stately way.

V

Praise for Thy long sustaining,
　That held her firm in aim
Ever to keep unwaning
　Our fair ancestral fame ;
Praise for the sweet compassion
　Which makes the wide world own
That Love's divinest fashion
　Is set from England's throne.

VI

LORD, as her realm lies truly
　'Neath an unsetting sun,
As earthly meed all duly
　Her stainless life hath won :
So when at last before Thee
　She lays her kingdom down,
CHRIST's One Light be her glory,
　CHRIST's Merit be her crown.　Amen.

One Wide Majestic Temple

I

ONE wide majestic temple,
  Our Realm, from sea to sea,
Spreads 'neath the dome of Heaven,
  And there, O GOD, do we—
One heart in myriad voices—
  Our lauds uplift to Thee.

II

Hear Thy great congregation,
  O LORD of all, we pray !
There in the deepening sunset—
  Here in the opening day—
Where norland tempests hurtle—
  Where tropic breezes play.

III

We praise Thee for a Monarch,
  The stateliest under sun ;
Yet for the tenderest Woman
  The Throne has ever won ;
For sympathy the truest ;
  For duty grandly done.

IV

Queen-maiden—Wife—and Mother,
  She nobly filled her place :
And, when one awful shadow
  Had veiled a while her face,
Thy saintly patience crowned her
  With holier, sweeter grace.

V

We praise Thee for Thy Worker,
  The true, the wise, the strong—
Thy Guardian of our freedom,—
  Thy Warder against wrong,—
Thy Sufferer, singing softly
  Life's solemn undersong.

VI

Through all her sacred service
  Her FATHER, SAVIOUR, FRIEND—
Through threescore years beside her
  To guide, console, defend—
LORD, bless Thine own Anointed
  On to the glorious end.   Amen.

O Lord of Lords

(General, or for Children's Use)

I

O Lord of lords, and of all kings The King,

To Thee with heart and voice Thy children sing

Their festal Alleluia.

II

For solemn trust of power, for grace of peace,

For island sowings to world-wide increase,

We sing our Alleluia.

III

For that Cross-Flag to every wind unfurled

Beneath a sun that sets not on our world,

We sing our Alleluia.

IV

For our Three-Realms-in-One, and Realms afar,

As deep responds to deep, and star to star,

We sing our Alleluia.

V

On Asian, Afric, Australasian shores,

Where Ocean, tuned to our great Anthem, roars,

Is sung our Alleluia.

VI

But now to Thee, our proudest songs above,
For Her, th' Anointed Lady of our love,
>> We sing our Alleluia.

VII

New voices, from fresh heart of song, we raise :
A high new note of joy now swells our praise
>> And wings our Alleluia.

VIII

For this new year that fronts her diadem
With threescore lustre in one matchless gem,
>> We sing our Alleluia.

IX

Great LORD of all, let this new light live on,
In our true love, till she shall hear anon
>> A sweeter Alleluia.

X

Till, past this fading life of days and years,
She wears Thy Love's immortal crown and hears
>> The endless Alleluia.   Amen.

All the Mountain Heights

(General, or for Children's Use)

I

ALL the mountain heights adorning,
  All th' horizons of the main
With new light, ascends the morning,
  Stateliest of Victoria's reign—
        GOD save the Queen.

II

Thrice enthroned![1] so thrice upon her
  Came th' anointing from above—
Youth of gladness, age of honour,
  And the highest grace of love—
        GOD save the Queen.

III

Seems not Time himself to love her?
  Dear liege-Lady of our Land—

[1] In 1837—in 1887—in 1897.

Years threescore have swept above her,
  Each with blessing in its hand—
        GOD save the Queen.

IV

GOD in springtide chose the maiden,
  Sealed her for His service long,
On to years with winter laden
  Made her stronger than the strong—
        GOD save the Queen.

V

On our old historic pages
  Now her name is shining clear;
Queen elect of all the ages,
  'Midst her peers without a peer—
        GOD save the Queen.

VI

Great in loneliness and sorrow
  As when gladness sunned her way,
Waiting the Divine To-morrow
  'Mid the duties of To-day—
        GOD save the Queen.

VII

Ring it out from tower and steeple !
Blazon it by flag unfurled !
She is loved of all her people :
She is honoured by the world :—
GOD save the Queen.

VIII

And we pray, who bow before Thee,
Thee her Master, Thee her Friend,
From this glory to Thy glory
Guide her, guard her to the end.
GOD save the Queen.   Amen.